I was ready for hostility, anger, bitter resentment, even blame, thought Casey.

Instead it was like they all knew she was going to turn up one day. Kindness and generosity seemed to emanate from Darcy. *Her big sister?*

"You're too nice to me," Casey said abruptly.

"Who could deny a goddess?" Troy pressed back in his chair, smiling his bold, tantalizing smile.

"It's settled, then," Darcy said, eyes sparkling. "Give us a call when you want to come home."

Never had Casey been so glad she had her sunglasses on. She, who never cried except on increasingly rare occasions when she was flooded by her nightmares, felt the sting of tears.

Home? Did she have a home? If she hadn't been such an undemonstrative person she would have put her arms around Darcy and hugged her.

Margaret Way takes great pleasure in her work and works hard at her pleasure. She enjoys tearing off to the beach with her family on weekends, loves haunting galleries and auctions and is completely given over to French champagne "for every possible joyous occasion." She was born and educated in the river city of Brisbane, Australia, and now lives within sight and sound of beautiful Moreton Bay.

MARGARET WAY

Marriage at Murraree

The
McIvor Sisters

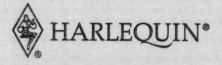

HARLEQUIN®

TORONTO • NEW YORK • LONDON
AMSTERDAM • PARIS • SYDNEY • HAMBURG
STOCKHOLM • ATHENS • TOKYO • MILAN • MADRID
PRAGUE • WARSAW • BUDAPEST • AUCKLAND

ISBN 0-373-18209-0

MARRIAGE AT MURRAREE

First North American Publication 2005.

Copyright © 2005 by Margaret Way, Pty., Ltd.

This edition published by arrangement with Harlequin Books S.A.

www.eHarlequin.com

Printed in U.S.A.

CHAPTER ONE

IF SHE hadn't landed on planet Mars, she didn't know where she was. The heat and the blinding glare! The colour of the desert sand was unbelievable, fiery-red, burnt-orange. It glowed like a furnace under the rich blue sky. The very *vastness* stunned her. The plains ran out to the horizon without anything to connect them to humans. It must seem the same to a sailor adrift on a great ocean she thought. Her trip was turning into quite an experience. The lack of *anything* except the land in all its savage glory was amazing. Space. Pure air. Freedom. In a place like this she might be able to regain her soul. These desert areas—and she realised she was only on the desert fringe—were seemingly barren except for the eternal porcupine grasses, the Spinifex. It had covered huge areas of her journey into Queensland's vast Outback. The legendary name, *The Never Never* was right on. She had never seen such a surreal landscape outside of a painting.

Brilliant red earth, cobalt vault, totally cloudless, large rounded clumps of Spinifex like giant pincushions scorched to a dull gold. In the distance the baffling mirage danced in waves, conjuring up alluring green oases with lots of lovely water. She could well understand how the early pioneers had followed it, never catching up. This had to be somewhere near the place the English explorer, Captain Charles Sturt had battled his way with horses in search of the inland sea. What had he called it? The Iron Region. Or maybe that was the Stony Desert named after him. Either way it was awesome country, with enormous drawing power.

Casey pulled off the dead straight road that went nowhere. Goodness knows why, she thought wryly, no one else was on it. She'd been travelling for days yet she'd hardly seen a soul. She turned off the ignition of her battered old ute and consulted her map again, resting it on the steering wheel. To be landed in this immense empty wilderness could turn out to be extremely hazardous. One wouldn't need to have a breakdown or run out of water. The glare alone was soporific. It had damned nearly put her to sleep. Of course the ancient ute had no air-conditioning and it was blazingly hot.

It was well she was tough. She had to be. No one had looked after her. She had lived hard. Born in a shack on the outskirts of a tropical town. Reared by a mother who hardly knew how to look after herself let alone a child. Then after her mother had died of a drug overdose, The Home. Bad, bad days. She'd endured that until she was sixteen when she left with nothing but searing memories. Truth was she had never had a real home anywhere.

You've got a lot to answer for, Jock McIvor.

Casey reckoned he'd be in hell and deservedly so.

There was nothing else to do but drive on, hoping Old Faithful would make it into the Three Rivers Country. For years she had heard mention of the Channel Country in the State's far South-West on the weather report. She hadn't taken much notice except to register it was darn *hot!* To her mind it sounded like the end of the earth. Only very recently had she learned it was the legendary home of the nation's cattle kings. The domain of men like Jock McIvor.

She had never known who her father was. The kids at school had given her hell about that. Her poor little mother had been a joke, the butt of many a sick prank. Kids were so cruel. Pretty as a picture but so overwhelmed by life her mother had eventually sought solace first in alcohol, then in drugs. She had once confessed to Casey she didn't want to live.

She hadn't. She'd OD'd at the grand old age of thirty-six. Casey had always blamed herself for not being able to protect her mother but then she was only a kid at the time. At eleven she'd been put into The Home. Plenty of kids there didn't have fathers or mothers, either. It wasn't unusual for parents to dump their kids or make life so unbearable for them even The Home was preferable.

Casey drove on. She figured she was two hundred kilometres west of her last stop, the bush town of Cullen Creek. She hadn't seen any creek, just a dry sandy bed someone told her in times of flood turned into a raging torrent. Hard to believe! As she'd gone in search of something to eat, the townspeople had stared at her like she'd stepped off a UFO that had landed in the main street. But at least they had given her a decent cup of tea and a plate of sandwiches made with freshly baked bread and plenty of ham and salad filling. A big apple and cinnamon muffin to follow and lots of advice about always letting someone know where she was heading in the Outback.

She hadn't told them where she was going. Her appearance alone had magnetised them. Probably her height and her red hair. Both had made her a target as a kid. "How's the weather up there, Agent Orange?" Even her mother had seemed to blame her for looking the way she did. At least her formidable height had saved her from a few batterings in The Home. She was good with her nails and her fists and her high kicking legs. The world was a dangerous place. She had found that out early.

Then six weeks ago, a blast from the past. An old friend of her mother's came into her life. Not by chance. Judith Harrison had gone to a great deal of trouble to track down first Casey's mother, then learning of her premature death, her only child. Judith Harrison it turned out had grown up with her mother and knew all about the family "tragedy". Casey had not known anything about it since it had never passed her mother's lips. Her poor little mother—at least they had loved one another—had been born into a well-to-do family. Casey had to have that explained to her. *Twice.* A woman who had lived with her child often below the breadline had come from a cushy background. The irony of it! Casey's grandparents had since died, no doubt leaving their small fortune to a retirement village for pampered cats. Judith had been her mother's friend from childhood, apparently consumed by guilt that she had never sought to contact Casey's mother after she stormed out of the parental home, cutting all ties.

It was on account of a man. It always was. A mystery man Casey's grandparents had never met yet instinctively feared. He had taken over their hitherto perfect daughter's life, making her a different person. When Casey had calmed down from the revelation her mother had come from a very comfortable home, Judith told her she had spotted her mother and her lover just once. Once was enough. A week later she had seen the man being interviewed on television.

His name was Jock McIvor. Swashbuckling cattle baron. A man with money to burn.

Jock McIvor, who it appeared short of DNA testing, was Casey's father. He couldn't be anything else. He was even taller than she was. After she had finally closed the door on a sobbing Judith Harrison, nevertheless de-lumbered of her burden, Casey had made it her business to read up everything she could about McIvor that paragon of sin; all the press clippings, accompanied by photographs. Judith Harrison hadn't lied. Handsome was too tame a word for him. The photographs were all in black and white so she didn't know his exact colouring except for what Judith Harrison had told her. He had a leonine shock of red-gold hair. He was very tall, probably six-four with sapphire eyes and a cleft in his chin. Casey had almost laughed. It fit her own colouring. She even had—in her case—a dimple in her chin. In no way had she resembled her dark haired, dark eyed mother who'd been five-three at most. The person she resembled obviously was the person who had seduced her naïve little mother, ultimately destroying her life.

A man without conscience. Jock McIvor.

Powerful, rich, probably dumping one woman

after the other, he had taken everything her mother could give him, then returned to his own world where pretty gullible little creatures like her mother didn't belong. By the time her mother found out she was pregnant she was on her own and a long way from home. Casey had no way of knowing what her mother had felt then but she must have been terrified with no one to turn to. She had alienated her parents in abandoning herself to her lover.

Only her lover, it turned out, had a wife and a baby. A baby called Darcy.

Jock McIvor, who should have had Dirty Rotten Scoundrel as a bumper sticker.

But he was dead. That was okay. The family was going to pay. Those McIvor women—she knew all about the other one, Courtney, who had arrived a couple of years after the first born Darcy—those *McIvor heiresses* as the Press dubbed them—were rolling in money. That struck Casey as being shockingly unfair. If she were McIvor's daughter and she didn't for a moment doubt that she was, wasn't she entitled to a stake? It was about time the poor and oppressed of this world had justice. Well she was poor enough to qualify but just let anyone try to oppress her. She'd had more than her fair share of that in The Home where all her survival skills had been tested.

She was probably traumatised. She had been sexually assaulted by The Cobra but he hadn't managed to rape her on account of the noise she made and a great kick that would have carried her far in soccer, sending him hurtling across the room. She was fourteen then, almost at her full height and as wiry as hell. That had sent a message to the others. Leave McGuire alone or she might be tempted to slug you or kick you in the balls. She never had much of an education. About two days at school and a smattering of the three R's she picked up at The Home where grade ten was about as good as it got. Could she ever forget even in her time two of the kids had committed suicide, unable to withstand the day in day out torment? She had prayed and prayed they had gone to a much better place....

For years Casey had been supporting herself singing for her supper. People really liked her in the pubs where she was starting to make a name for herself as a singer-songwriter. She had a good voice for country and she liked to think plenty of talent on the guitar. One of her boyfriends, a really nice guy—yes, there were a few out there—had taught her. He had even passed over his own expensive guitar saying when he heard *her* he realised he shouldn't play any more. She'd even managed to finish her formal education to Leaving Certificate. Emboldened by the results, she had taken up various courses at an Adult Learning institute, even basic French. It made her feel cultured. On the purely practical side she'd signed on for a get-to-know-your-car course where she'd outshone most of the guys. Heck, she was as good as any A Grade garage mechanic, which was probably why the ute was still running.

Twenty minutes later she saw on a slight rise set well back from the road, a fairly impressive dwelling for this or any other neck of the woods. A homestead of some kind? Though she leaned forwards peering through the windshield she couldn't see a solitary goat let alone a herd of cattle. It even had trees around it. Desert oaks. She'd become familiar with them. Several towering gums. A couple of palms. The house was two storey, built of rose coloured bricks finished off with wide verandahs, white cast-iron balustrades and white lattice treillage. What in the world was a quite handsome house doing in the middle of nowhere?

"You're seeing things, Casey girl," she mumbled to herself. Her heart missed a beat as a large stone flew up from the road and hit the windshield at a point close to her head. At various intervals on her long journey she had seen piles of glass at the side of the road marking the spots where some traveller had struck trouble. Mercifully her windscreen remained intact, but she would like to take on more water. The house didn't look deserted. It looked lived-in. She could see a big galvanised iron water tank off to one side and a few outbuildings at the back. Surely a weary traveller could beg a container of water? Outback people were supposed to be hospitable. On the other hand she might run into some ornery character totting a .22. Nothing life dished up surprised her.

Okay, let's see! Casey took the gravelled side road that led to the house. She wasn't counting on a gate. I mean just how many people came calling? Nevertheless she got out to open it and closed it securely after her once the ute was inside. Maybe a bunch of cows was out back planning a stampede?

Not cows. A cattle dog, with the distinctive blue speckled coat and dark tan markings. She knew what it was. A Queensland Blue Heeler bred especially for droving and rounding up cattle. It came skittling around a corner of the house barking its head off, probably determined to make amends for having been taking a nap.

"Hey, fella!" she called to it, standing her ground. "What's *your* problem? I'm not a bad person. I'm here for water."

The bluey must have liked the sound of her voice. It stopped barking and came right up to her as though eager to clear up any misunderstandings.

"Hi, there, what's your name?" She bent to pat it. She liked animals better than people and they liked her. There was a collar around its neck with a name tag.

"Rusty!" She chuckled. "Is that your name? Howya goin', Rusty? You're a clever boy. How about showing me up to the house?"

She could have sworn the dog smiled.

She rapped on the solid timber front door. No one came.

"Damn, Rusty!" The owner had to be away. They had probably taken a run into the town, which on her map was Koomera Crossing. She kept talking away to the dog to prove her good intentions. The front door was offset by brilliant stained glass panels, fan lights and sidelights, in the style she had learned was Art Nouveau. She had been starved of beauty. Now she was making up for lost time. She was taking a closer look, one hand resting gently against the front door when the door suddenly gave. It swung open and she was left looking into a generous entrance hall illuminated by the brilliant sunlight. It had an unusual floor of alternating light and dark boards. There was little furniture beyond a single painting hanging above a small dark timber console.

"Hello, there," she called. "Anyone at home?" But if anyone was at home, surely they would have heard Rusty's barking.

Afterwards she never knew why she walked in

but everything about the place was irresistible. Rusty followed her, making not the slightest attempt to nip at her heels.

Casey laughed. "Some watchdog you are." She gave him another pat while he looked back at her with an eager, expectant face as if soon they'd be outside playing catch. Obviously Rusty had retired. "Since I'm here, I suppose it's okay if I fill my container." She went back to the ute to get it with the cattle dog padding along happily at her side. "Rusty, you old dog, you like women. I wonder if you'd be so nice if I were a man?" Probably not. Men were such threatening creatures. Women weren't.

By the time she filled the big container to the top it was heavy. She lowered it to the floor and then, because she was so much enjoying being inside such a house, she decided to take a quick look around. She wouldn't go upstairs. She felt sure she shouldn't, but there was no harm in taking a look around the ground floor and out the back. Rusty didn't mind. It was a large house but the furnishings were austere.

The back door was open as well. Obviously the occupier was very trusting. Not that there was anything worth taking. Rusty thinking she might be about to have a look outside, bounded down the short flight of steps, looking back up at her.

It was then she was caught from behind, her arms

pinned and hauled behind her back. She had heard no footsteps. Nothing. There was the power of untold strength in the grip.

"What the hell are you up to, cowboy?" A man's voice ground out. He kicked the back door shut so Rusty couldn't come to her aid.

That was it! No one manhandled *her*. The fingers that encircled her wrists were like bands of steel. She could just imagine the rest of him but she wasn't about to cringe or beg for mercy. Was there no place on earth there wasn't violence?

She felt a surge of adrenalin, heaving with all her might to loosen the powerful grip. She was far from being a weak woman. She was strong. She'd worked out four times a week at the gym. She lifted weights. Add to that she had taken karate lessons at which she'd proved a natural. She succeeded in freeing herself to the extent one of her hands came loose. That was all she needed. She whirled, ready to defend herself with ugly memories flashing before her eyes. Under attack, she took two quick steps forward, raised her right leg to chest height then drove the ball of her foot at him in a snap kick.

It should have connected but at the last minute he rapidly sidestepped. Immediately she spun, abandoning the idea of another snap kick he might have been expecting for a good old-fashioned sock at his jaw. Bewdy! She heard with satisfaction his grunt as his neck snapped back.

Next things, in under a couple of seconds she was flat on her back, gasping for breath, with her assailant standing over her. She reacted swiftly, rolling away across the carpet runner. One strike each.

"You're not going to hurt *me,* you bastard!" She was out of a crouch, back on her feet, fully in control of her body, her mind locked into self-defence. There was no place for panic. She wasn't going down without a fight.

Trust no man. Your life could depend upon it.

He was taller than she was. Maybe by three or four inches. Rugged and rangy. He was young, too, under thirty. Good tanned skin lay taut over carved bones, thick golden-brown hair, sun-streaked blond. For a space of a breath she thought, gold eyes. Who had *gold* eyes? She couldn't feel a rapist's aura. Instead he was saying tersely, "Get a grip, girl. I'm not going to hurt you." His expression was startled.

It took a few moments for what he was saying to sink through her consciousness.

"Who *are* you?" she demanded, maintaining her aggressive stance. At the same time she manoeuvred herself to the back door so she could let Rusty in.

"God!" he exhaled softly. "I had no idea you were a woman." His voice abruptly hardened. "So what do you mean, who am *I?* I'm asking the questions around here. Who are *you?* What are you doing here and what do you want? Look, it's okay." He held up his hands. "How long have you been a karate cum prize fighter?"

"As long as guys like you are around!" Her face was still alight with anger, her sapphire eyes blazing. "Maybe I shouldn't be in here, but I knocked. The door gave. I thought it would be all right if I filled my water container. It's in the kitchen. What did you think I was going to do? Pinch your lousy possessions?"

"Could be," he returned, a faint smile on his generous mouth.

"I'm going to let Rusty in," she said, like Rusty was a trained killer. She flattened herself against the back door then opened it. This guy was tough. Very tough. She saw that now. There wouldn't be a woman alive who could match his physical strength. Seconds later Rusty was inside the house, exhausted from having run back and forth finding the door locked against him.

"Sit, boy," her assailant gave the clipped order. Rusty sat.

Of course! It had to be *his* dog, though she doubted very much he could get the cattle dog to turn on her.

"Your name please?" he asked, suddenly as formal as a policeman.

"Casey McGuire."

"No doubt of the mad McGuire clan?" He examined her from head to toe. Far from being some young guy she was all *femaleness*.

"No clan," she informed him shortly. "I'm an orphan."

"I imagine your family prefer it that way. So what are you doing around here, Casey McGuire?"

"Drivin' through, if it's any of your business. This your house?"

"In a manner of speaking, but I don't live here. This house is at the disposal of our resident school master. It's a few kilometres out of town but he doesn't mind."

"Doesn't he ever lock his doors?" she asked.

"He will from now on," he informed her. "But as you say, there's nothing much to take. I apologise for manhandling you. I mistook you for some vagrant out to make trouble."

"Right!" she said firmly. "Now you know different. I don't apologise for slugging you. You asked for it."

He laughed, stroking a hand along his strong jaw where a dark red mark was still visible. "The fact your hat fell off gave you the element of surprise, so don't take too much credit. How many guys I wonder have a torrent of fiery hair tumbling down their back? How long did it take to grow it?"

"So what's *your* name," she replied, totally ignoring his smart aleck question. Yet all the while he was studying her intently, a small frown between his bronze brows.

"Connellan. Troy Connellan. My dad owns Vulcan Plains about 100 K's west of here. I had to come into town so I decided to take a run out here to check on a few things. I won't mention to Phil Carson—that's the new headmaster—you were snooping around his place."

She coloured. "I'm sorry. It's hard to explain. I was just enjoying the house. And Rusty's company." She clicked her fingers and the blue speckled dog came to her, showing its pleasure at a few pats on the head.

"Don't be a fool, Rusty," Troy Connellan chided. "He might look the picture of a sweet natured dog but I've seen Rusty hold quite a few people at bay."

"I'm good with animals," she said offhandedly. "So you believe me?"

"I have to put a stop to those right hooks," he answered sarcastically. "Yeah, I believe you. We got off to a bad start. Where are you heading?"

She shrugged. "I'm going to stop off at the town. Koomera Crossing?"

"Right." He nodded slowly, still intently sizing her up. There was nothing lecherous about it. The considerable interest wasn't on that account.

"Then I'm heading out to McIvor country. Murraree. That's the name of the station, isn't it?"

"Right again." He narrowed his eyes. "You're a relative of Jock's?"

"You could say that."

"I hope you know he's dead?"

"So I've heard. But not the end of story."

"You've got me intrigued, Ms McGuire."

Something about him sent an unwelcome self-awareness crackling along her nerves. "Look, I'm a busy woman." She said it through her teeth. "You knew Jock McIvor?"

"Lady, everyone knew Jock McIvor," he said laconically. "You ever so slightly resemble him."

"Do I now." She picked up her cream Akubra and rammed it back on her head. All day her hair had been pleated for coolness, now she let it fall loose.

"Have you told the girls you're coming?" He made a rough mocking sound like a snort.

She looked at him, thinking suddenly he was extraordinarily good-looking if you liked big dramatic hunks. He had strong distinctive features and a bump at the bridge of his aquiline nose, probably from an old break. The eyes were as gold as a jungle cat's, thickly lashed. "This is gonna be a big surprise," she drawled.

"I bet. Who the hell *are* you?"

"As I said before, none of your business, Connellan. I'll collect my container and be on my way. Have a nice day."

She couldn't stop him. He walked with her to the ute.

"You're expecting to get to Murraree in this old wreck?" he enquired, standing back to admire it.

"This old wreck has served me faithfully," she told him tartly.

"We do have a policeman in the town. Would it pass a road worthy test?"

"You're joking. Who the hell would care around here?"

"You'd be surprised. The fact it takes time and money to go after irresponsible idiots who find themselves broken down in the Outback doesn't seem to bother you."

"Look, buster!" She stuck her hands on her hips, adopting her aggressive stance. "I'm a mechanic. This here ute mightn't look pretty but it's well maintained. It's not gonna break down, got it?"

"Boy do you have a chip on your shoulder." He gave a white smile, the corners of his mouth curling up.

Fascinating. She was starting to get uncomfortable with the fact she was finding him attractive. "I don't like being called an irresponsible idiot."

He gave a mocking bow. "I was generalising, dear girl."

"I'm not your dear girl. I'm not a girl at all. I'm a *woman*."

"And an excellent specimen." He gave another wide smile. "Could I interest you in a cup of coffee back in town?"

"Not likely." This guy was getting under her skin faster than a splinter. "How far on is Murraree?"

"Not far as the crow flies. Darn near three hours by road. I suggest you don't drive after dark."

"Why is that. Do you think the dark might make me jumpy?" she jeered.

"*You?* No. That was some punch. I'm just glad the snap kick never connected. There are kangaroos on the road. They're as dumb as they come. I don't think your old ute would stand up to a front end collision. I travel with a bull bar."

"I take it that's your 4WD beyond the gate. What did you do, pole vault the fence?"

"I wanted to surprise you. At least you closed the gate behind you. Country girl."

She shook her head. "I've never been to the Outback in my life."

His bronze brows lifted. "Jock never invite you?"

"I never had the pleasure of meeting Jock McIvor."

"But you're a relation?"

She laughed, despite herself. "The evidence seems to be mounting up. Do you know the McIvor heiresses?"

"Darcy, yes. But the younger one, Courtney, stayed in Brisbane with her mother. She's only recently come back. I haven't had the pleasure as yet. I've been managing one of our outstations in the Territory."

"*One* of…" she scoffed. "You don't get to be as cocky as you unless Daddy happens to be a rich old cattle baron."

"You're just jealous." He shrugged. "Anyway you don't know the amount of rubbish I have to put with."

"And I couldn't care less. Now would you mind taking your arm off my car. I have to be on my way to this Koomera Crossing. The last town I pulled in every last damned citizen was all eyes. You would have thought I'd come from another planet."

"More likely every last damned person was struck by your extraordinary resemblance to Jock McIvor. It's kinda startling. You've even got the cleft chin."

"Make that a dimple." She slipped behind the wheel. "Could you do me a favour and open the gate?"

"How could you leave Rusty behind?" he asked, amused by the way the cattle dog had taken to her.

"He's your dog, not mine. I suppose you dumped him on the schoolteacher."

"Fella wanted a bit of protection."

She laughed. "It would be fair to say Rusty is a push-over."

"Or you could melt metal?"

Casey felt heat rush through her veins. This conversation had gone far enough. "I thought *you* were the one who behaved like a savage." She swung away.

"Look, I thought you were an intruder, okay?"

"I'm glad I wasn't. Are you going to open the gate?"

"Yes, ma'am." He gave a mocking salute. "If you stay on in town I might see you there."

"Not if I see you first," she called sweetly. "Bye, Rusty!" She waited until he had opened the gate fully, before revving away in a cloud of red dust and flying gravel. Rusty followed, in hot pursuit. Just as she started to worry, Connellan let out a whistle so piercing Rusty got the message and reluctantly returned home.

More amazement at Koomera Crossing. More long considering stares. More unsolicited advice not to attempt to travel after dusk, which made it even more dangerously irresistible, but she wasn't a complete fool. She booked into the pub for the night. She could start out fresh in the morning.

By seven o'clock she was starving. She felt sure the pub didn't run to room service but if she went down to the dining room she might run into Troy Connellan. Just the thought of him made the adrenalin kick in. His wasn't a soothing presence. In fact, he was particularly challenging. She could still feel that steely grip on her. She supposed he had every reason to think she was a lanky young man from the back. There was her height, her long legs and her dusty cowboy garb. Her hair—what had he called it?—a fiery torrent, was pushed under her hat. So his daddy owned the schoolmaster's house. He owned a place called Vulcan Plains and another station in the Northern Territory. Daddy had to be a rich man. A cattle baron.

Spare me from them.

Hunger got the better of her. There was a lot of her to fill. She prettied herself up with a fine cotton shirt the colour of her eyes and brand-new designer jeans, tight as leggings, slinging one of her very fancy belts around her waist. This was the sort of outfit she adopted in the pubs when she sang. People seemed to like it. Her hair she brushed until it crackled and left it to hang loose over her shoulders and down her back in deep thick waves. McIvor's hair. She sighed and a flush of anger appeared in her cheeks. A few things he had passed on to her. As a child she had wondered where she got her red curls from. Her mother's hair had been dark and glossy until she started not taking care of herself. Her mother had never forgotten McIvor but he had forgotten her overnight. Had her mother ever tried to contact him to tell him about the pregnancy? Casey never knew. He might have sent money or advised her mother to have an abortion. He would pay for it. He was a married man.

Her poor little mother had a higher morality.

She was hardly settled in her chair before a plump, middle-aged woman reminiscent of someone's mother on a sit-com came up to her, beaming. "I thought it was. You're Casey McGuire, aren't you? I'm a fan of yours. I've heard you sing back in Brisbane and the Gold Coast. I'm on holiday staying with my niece. She's over there." She gestured towards a table. "Dee Walker, that's my name." She held out her hand.

What else could a girl do. Casey shook it. "Thanks for the kind words, Dee, but I won't be doing any singing around here."

Dee's double chin quivered as if she might cry. "Not even if I asked you? Folks would love it."

Casey stared up at the woman's plum-hued hair. "I'm like you, Dee, I'm on vacation." Dee wore a plum lipstick as well.

Dee wasn't the sort of person who took no for an answer. She leaned her hands on the table. "Look, I've set myself the little task of getting you to sing. I bet hubby I could."

"Dee, I'm about to order. I'm very hungry."

"Later then?" Dee was nothing if not persistent.

It had worked countless times in the past. People just folded before they got a migraine.

Casey wasn't one of them. She was about to put a stop to Dee, only a voice she knew breathed over her shoulder. "Hey, sorry I'm late!" Next minute Troy Connellan dropped an audacious kiss on her cheek before taking the chair opposite her.

"Oh, I'm intruding," Dee Walker said, looking pleasantly flustered.

"Nice to meet you, Dee," Casey gave her a big bright smile. "Bye now."

Dee left reluctantly while Connellan rolled his eyes. "Don't tell me. She wanted to know if that hot hair was real?"

"You've heard about wigs in the sticks?"

"Hell, yes. What did she want?"

For some unknown reason she told him. "She wanted me to sing a song."

"Imagine that!" One bronze eyebrow shot up. "What are we talking about here? Grand opera, pop, rock and roll, maybe the blues?" He had already noted her speaking voice, low and rich, full of sexy modulations.

She looked at him through narrowed, hostile eyes. "I'm sorry I told you."

He shook his head. "Contrary to what you may believe, any one of those styles is possible. You have a voice people would want to listen to. So did

Jock come to think of it. I don't think I've ever heard anyone spin a yarn like McIvor. That voice of his could weave spells."

"Can we leave McIvor out of this?" she asked sharply

"Sounds like you don't have a good opinion of him?"

"Go on. Dig a bit further," she challenged.

Again he shook his head. "I'm here for a nice chat and to have a good dinner. Have you ordered yet?"

"Dee got in the way," she said sarcastically.

"Allow me." He held up a hand. Immediately a pretty young waitress with dyed platinum hair curling around her head, hurried to their table.

"Yes, Troy?"

He smiled up at her. "How are things with you, Debby?"

"Just the same as when you left, Troy. Pretty tame, but I have dreams."

It looked very much like Connellan was one of them, Casey thought, sitting back and listening to the exchange. It went on for a minute more before they ordered. Fresh barramundi had arrived from the Gulf, so what else? French fries, green salad on the side.

"Thanks, Debby." Connellan handed her the menus. "We'll let you know if we want dessert."

"Thank *you*, Troy," she said, eyes glowing, cheeks pink.

"One of your girlfriends?" Casey asked. "Or not high enough up the social scale?"

"Debby's just a kid," he frowned. His white shirt revealed a glimpse of broad bronzed torso, a gold ring in his ear would have finished the look off perfectly. Even his thick hair curled up from his collar.

"A kid with a crush," Casey pointed out." Whereas you're *exactly* the age Debby is attracted to. You did a good job making her want to grow up. *Fast.*"

"I don't know what you're talking about," he said. Another signal of the hand. "What's it to be?" He turned back to Casey. "Beer or wine? I guess a glass of wine wouldn't kill me."

"Perhaps you should go sit at another table?" she suggested sweetly.

"Don't be like that, McGuire. Waiter's coming. What's it to be?"

"A nice crisp Riesling," she said.

The generous mouth compressed. "If they've got it. Crisp Riesling drinkers don't come in all that often."

"Try them," she said.

The owner of the pub, a pleasant-looking man with bright blue eyes took her request very seriously. He smiled their way and waved a hand, indicating he had just what she wanted in stock.

Not only that, the bottle arrived nicely chilled.

Troy poured. "You're going to drink this whole bottle by yourself?" he mocked.

"If that's okay with you." She gave a uncaring shrug. "I'll have as little or as much as I like. Who the heck asked you to join me, may I ask?"

"No use glowering at me," he said. "I was rescuing you from Dee. You come on real strong, don't you McGuire?"

"Hasn't stopped you coming back for more. And who said you could call me McGuire?"

"I distinctly recall your calling me Connellan. What's good for the goose, etc., etc. What do you say we call it a truce while we polish off the barramundi?"

"Fine. I plan on going to bed early."

It wasn't to turn out that way. The main course was so delicious they followed it with a chocolate mousse then coffee.

"Who's paying, by the way?" he asked.

"You're wasting your time if you're trying to take a rise out of me."

"I just can't make out if you actually smile or not." He looked boldly into her eyes.

"Wouldn't you just *love* to tell me it's just like McIvor's."

"Jock McIvor was renowned for his sexual prowess," he said. "Part of the appeal was his flashing smile."

"He must have exercised it a lot," she said contemptuously. "Don't look for it from me. I had a tough childhood."

"Really?" He leaned closer. "Turns out so did I. Maybe we can compare notes? Let's order another coffee seeing you're paying."

She nodded. For one reason only, or so she told herself. The short black had been very good. She'd only had two glasses of wine, so she'd take the rest of the bottle up to her room. Maybe have another drop to help her sleep. Alcohol wasn't going to be her downfall. She could take it or leave it.

Five minutes later Dee descended on them again. This time wearing elaborate spectacles. She seemed tremendously excited. "I've waited and waited," she announced. "But now you're finished. There's a young man here with a guitar. Says his name is John Denver. Joking of course. He said he'd lend you his guitar if you would sing. I've spoken to the publican. Such a nice man! He said his customers would love it."

Casey hoped her smile was okay. "Fact is, Dee, I don't usually sing *after* a meal." She had numerous times but not professionally.

"If I were you," Connellan chipped in. "I'd get it over."

"Why can't you just keep out of it?" Casey fired.

"I'd *lurve* to hear you," he drawled. "Never let it be said I don't enjoy the finer things in life."

"Oh, please, please," Dee added, for good measure putting her hands together in a little clap. "Look here comes Johnny with his guitar."

"Wonder it's not Elvis," Connellan murmured, giving her a gold-gleaming glance full of humour. "Clearly you're caught!"

Casey took the tiny stage to much applause and more than a few loud whistles. She'd been so engrossed crossing swords with Troy Connellan she really hadn't registered the amount of interest she'd been getting. If people whispered among themselves at Cullen Creek, at Koomera Crossing speculation was rife. The consensus of opinion. "Got to be one of Jock's!"

Dee, electing herself compere of the night, took it upon herself to make the introductions.

"Please make welcome, Casey McGuire, all the way from Brisbane. You're in for a treat, folks."

More applause. More loud catcalls.

Casey took a minute to fine tune the guitar. Perfect pitch was quite rare she'd found and she had it. She decided on a sad ballad. One she had written herself. Most of her songs were sad. This one was some kind of memorial to her mother. Someone had turned on a spotlight and it shone on her.

She didn't need the mike but the publican hurried to switch it on, while someone else drew up a high chair for her to play sitting down if she wished. Anyone would have thought she was a rock star, she was getting so much attention.

"Song for Marnie," she said, simply, looking out into the now crowded dining room. Where had everyone come from? The dining room had only been a little over half full.

Totally focused, she sat on the high stool unconscious of the image she created, strumming the introduction. Then when all was perfectly quiet, she began to sing....

Troy Connellan, rebel with good cause, found himself almost unbearably moved. She had a beautiful voice. He didn't know what category. Mezzo, contralto, it wasn't soprano. It was coming from some sad place deep inside her. Low and melodious, filled with emotion. She had wonderful control. Not only that, he had never heard the guitar sound so darned *good*. Her long elegant fingers caressed the strings, really made them sound. She was a true musician. Confrontational with him—he had to admit he'd gone out of his way to cause a little friction—when she sang of this Marnie her voice was heartbreakingly *sad*. She couldn't be lesbian could she? He rejected that. He'd had enough experience to know there was something sexual going on beneath their sparring. The lyrics seemed to tell him tragic Marnie could be her mother. She'd said she was an orphan and he'd mocked her. He was sorry now.

He began to think of another star-crossed woman. His own mother, Elizabeth. Of the great love between them. But his mother was dead. She and a family friend had been caught in a flash flood on the station. Rumour had it his mother and their friend, his godfather, had been having a forbidden affair. His mother had been so beautiful who wouldn't have fallen in love with her? His father was a very jealous man. Jealous of his beautiful mother. Jealous of him. He saw his only son as a rival and directed very real conflicts his way. It was all done on purpose. His father knew perfectly well what he was doing to Troy, at the same time as he heaped lavish gifts and affection on his sister, Leah. A new twist on the Oedipal dislocations.

This McGuire woman was simply *stunning* though she didn't seem to know it. Okay, she was very tall. Too tall for a woman, six feet, but not too tall for him. In the spotlight her magnificent Titian hair glittered like fairy gold. She had flawless milky-white skin. No freckles. He wondered how she'd missed out on them. Her long lithe body was decidedly feminine, incredibly fluid and infinitely sexy. And the length of those legs! They could have stretched to Cape York. He remembered as intimidating as he might first have appeared to her, she was ready and able to fight back. Unfortunately he'd made the huge mistake thinking she was some young guy snooping around. The battered old ute had given him a bum steer. What woman in her right mind drove such a bucket load of trouble?

What terrible times had Casey McGuire seen? What had provided the basis for the song? He was convinced she'd suffered to be able to sing with such depths. She'd told him she'd had a tough childhood. That made two of them. It had taken him forever to realize his father had been jealous of him even as a boy. It had much to do with his mother's special love for him and he for her.

After Casey finished there was total quiet in the room. It lasted for long moments as though the audience was unwilling to let the singer and the song drift away. Then the room erupted.

"More…more!"

A thunder of applause, this time no whistles perhaps out of respect, a muffled drumming of the feet, others stood up. A tourist with a plummy Pommy voice shouted, "Bravo!"

The singer, herself, seemed to come to, slowly as if breaking out of a trance.

Troy for his part was still trapped in the song's power and the sad memories it evoked.

Nothing could be clearer. Casey McGuire had many songs to sing and many stories to tell. No wonder she was heading for McIvor country. He'd take a bet on it. That's where she belonged.

Casey started into an encore. Upbeat, hand clapping, exciting. It drew a big response from her audience.

Casey McGuire, Goddess of Song.

CHAPTER TWO

Murraree Station

THE PEACE of that hot, languorous afternoon was disturbed by quite a commotion. An early model utility covered in red dust had entered the main compound, making speedy, ear splitting progress up the drive. By the time it rattled to a halt at the base of the homestead's front steps they were all standing wondering who the heck it was. Darcy and Curt were at the balustrade, Marian and Peter out of their chairs, Adam standing tall at Courtney's side startled by something in her expression.

"What's wrong?"

Shaken by premonition, Courtney put a hand to her throat. "I have a feeling this is serious," she said.

"Serious? In what way?" Adam stared down at her golden head.

"We'll soon find out."

Typically Curt took charge. He called out to the

driver using only enough authority as was necessary. "Hello there! What do you want?" It wasn't usual this kind of charge to the front door. No one they knew drove such a vehicle, either. For one thing it looked like it should have been in a wrecker's yard, but at least it hadn't caught fire.

In front of Courtney's mesmerised eyes a very tall young woman slid from the driver's seat, banging the door rigorously. Probably she had to, to make it shut.

"Which one of you is Darcy?" she demanded to know in a rich caustic voice. She moved towards them sweeping off her wide-brimmed cream Akubra. Immediately a magnificent unbound fiery mane tumbled down her back. She had eyes the colour of sapphires.

Four people saw the resemblance at once but no one said a word. They were temporarily struck dumb. Darcy, Courtney, their mother Marian, Curt, Darcy's fiancé, the love of her life.

Some things in life one couldn't evade, Courtney thought.

"Cat got your tongue?" The young woman addressed Darcy, who stood frozen. She flashed a familiar brilliant smile that held a world of challenge. "Hi, I'm Casey. Jock McIvor was my dad. Now are you going to let me up?"

Courtney looked quickly at her elder sister, waiting for Darcy to respond.

Darcy did, keeping the tremendous shock from her voice. "By all means, join us, Casey whatever-your-name," she responded levelly. "Looks like you've come a long way?"

Casey gave the dark haired young woman on the verandah another smile. "Indeed I have. Thanks a lot."

What should they do now, Courtney wondered, looks passing quickly around. Once on the verandah the statuesque red-head made a bee-line for her. "And you couldn't be anyone else but Courtney, the younger sister. Hi, there, Courtney. You're as pretty as a picture." She put out her hand and Courtney, feeling very odd took it, thinking she'd have to check her fingers afterwards. That was some grip for a woman.

"You have proof you're Jock McIvor's daughter?" Adam spoke for the first time, using his smooth dispassionate lawyer's voice.

"Hell, do I need it?" The goddess fixed him with a blue stare.

She sounded so much like Jock, *looked* so much like Jock, Marian sat back down in her chair, feeling a light sweat break out over her body. Just how long had Jock been faithful to her? Answer. Never. Jock had made quite a sideline out of sleeping with other women.

"And you must be Marian, McIvor's wife?" Casey advanced on Marian who was looking a bit pale.

"She was." Darcy did the answering. From the expression on her face, Marian was marooned in a sea of unhappy memories. "As you correctly deduced, that's my mother." For the first time a flicker of anger showed in Darcy's voice, but she made the introductions. "My mother's husband Peter Owens, my fiancé, Curt Berenger, and our friend and family lawyer, Adam Maynard."

"In short, everybody," Casey said, sounding brisk and assured. "So will someone offer me a drink?"

"Why not!" Darcy shrugged, finding for all her air of challenge she somehow *liked* this strange young woman who might or might not be her half sister. She was shockingly like Jock. She even talked like him. "Perhaps a meal?" Darcy suggested.

"That would be lovely." Casey broke out another smile, drenched in sunshine. "I haven't eaten since breakfast. That was at Koomera Crossing. I'd have been here a lot earlier, only I had a few problems with the ute I had to fix."

"You fixed it yourself?" Courtney who had no talent for fixing anything mechanical was amazed.

"Who else?" The goddess shrugged carelessly. "I take pleasure in keeping it running."

"So why have you come here, Casey?" Curt asked, suddenly in Guardian mode.

She flashed that startling blue glance at him. "Why, to get to know my family of course."

"But Casey," Adam said gently, "we don't know that you *are* family. Despite the remarkable resemblance, Darcy and Courtney have to have proof. We all do."

"Sure, you're a lawyer," Casey said. "Just wait till you hear my story."

They did over dinner. After their visitor downed a cold beer, Darcy had shown her to a recently refurbished guest room, leaving her to get the dust and the grime of her journey off her and settle in.

"I always knew this was going to happen," Darcy confided to Courtney. "It has an inevitability about it. Dad had so many affairs. The only thing I got wrong was I thought it would be a son."

"Watch out, there's still time," Courtney warned. "Any number could pop out of the woodwork. If Casey has waited until now, she probably read about Dad's death in the papers. You know what that means, don't you?"

"Sure." Darcy didn't sound worried. "She wants money. But she has to prove her identity first."

"She looks pretty authentic to me," Courtney said. "Fact is, I kind of like her though she's not the sweetest young woman I've ever met. And that handshake! For a minute I was frightened she was going to toss me over her shoulder."

"She could do it, too." Darcy's aquamarine eyes

looked into the middle distance. "I have the feeling Casey has done it hard. But she's never let anything stop her. I figure she's a fighter."

"So do I," Courtney agreed with some feeling. "You don't think she's here to threaten us?"

"Let's wait and see," Darcy advised.

"Sorry I couldn't run to a dress," Casey said, eyeing the other women. Pretty as a picture, Courtney had on something ultra-feminine in a lovely shade of violet. It floated on the air. Darcy, who was unmistakably a beauty, wore an outfit not unlike her own. A silk shirt over lean designer jeans. Casey loved the way Darcy carried her tall slender body with confident grace. She looked as at home in her body as Casey was in hers. Marian, the mother—probably Courtney would look just like her at the same age—hardly looked old enough to have two grown up daughters. She, too, was a pretty sight, calm and gentle with tender blue eyes. As a type she wasn't unlike her own mother. A cloud drifted over Casey's face. Her mother, too, had been a very pretty woman before poverty, unhappiness and the drugs she couldn't live without had changed all that.

As for the men! Berenger, the Outback aristocrat. *Very* impressive. Maynard, the lawyer, suave as James Bond. Peter, the second husband, a nice man but beside McIvor in his prime, hardly worth looking at.

It surprised Casey little five-feet-two-and-a-bit Courtney was the cook. And a very good cook as it turned out. They ate well and deliciously. Casey didn't peck at her food daintily like Marian, who seemed to her a fragile person. She tucked in because she was hungry. She was always hungry since she'd made her escape from The Home. At any time she led a very active life. Her long journey into the Back O'Beyond had been exhausting. They left her alone until the main course of melt-in-the-mouth spiced loin of lamb with pine nuts served over a bed of spinach was taken away and little strawberry jellies with ice cream were brought in. Then the inquisition started just as she expected.

"When did you first find out Jock McIvor was your father?" Maynard asked, his keen dark eyes sweeping over her. "Did your mother tell you?"

"No, she didn't," she said briskly.

"You have your birth certificate?"

"I didn't think I needed one since I'm so obviously here," she answered facetiously.

"You need your birth certificate for many things, Casey," Darcy intervened quietly. "Why don't you tell us your story in your own words."

Casey finished her strawberry jelly first. It was very refreshing. "It's not a pretty story," she said.

Nothing was pretty around our father, Courtney thought.

"You don't need Peter and me here," Marian spoke in a wobbly voice, looking uncertainly around the table. This stunning-looking creature might well resent their presence. Casey McGuire had a combative air about her. Marian was much more at home with a sweetness of manner like her beloved Courtney.

"Mumma, please stay." Courtney put out a staying hand.

"Very well, dear."

As she spoke Casey could see their faces change. She told them about her early life in far North Queensland. She spoke about her mother with a tightened throat. She could see that upset them. She skimmed over The Home, her voice emotionless. She told them how she'd set about getting an education. Of the courses she had taken, the jobs that included waitressing, cleaning, drawing beer in pubs, unloading trucks, working in nurseries where she'd picked up quite a lot of information about horticulture, finally her career as a singer-songwriter.

"Is this your future? Is this what you want to do?" Courtney asked, sparked by interest. Listening to her speak, there was no doubt Casey McGuire had a voice.

"Maybe." Casey shrugged. "I'm getting to like the writing more than the singing."

"So when did you find out Jock was your father if your mother didn't tell you?" Curt asked, disturbed by her story. Especially what she *hadn't* said about the orphanage. That in itself spoke volumes.

"An old friend of my mother's," Casey answered. "It seems she'd been suffering from the guilts for years. She knew of my mother's affair and her leaving home in disgrace. Some time later she saw my mother and Jock McIvor together. A few days after that she saw him again on television, being interviewed about something in the bush. She put two and two together. It must have cost her a big effort because she took years and years before she decided to track down my mother. By then, of course, my mother was dead."

"As was Jock," Curt said quietly. "The way you tell it it's impossible not to believe your story, Casey—a very sad story—but it doesn't actually prove Jock was your father."

"Dig him up," she suggested, her heart slamming. She'd just told them Jock McIvor had destroyed her mother's life.

Marian looked appalled. "How old are you, Casey?" She swallowed on emotion.

"Twenty-four. A few months younger than Courtney here."

It fitted, Marian thought dismally. Jock had had no time for her when she was pregnant. Not with

Darcy. Not with Courtney. She recalled his numerous city trips at those times.

"I've done a lot of research on Jock McIvor," Casey was saying. "He was a serial adulterer. Sorry if I offend anybody." She didn't look sorry. In fact she looked like she'd desperately needed to say it.

"We don't need the late Mr McIvor to prove paternity," Adam said, scanning their visitor closely but with discretion. "We can compare your DNA with that of Darcy's or Courtney's. What is it you want, Ms McGuire?"

Casey turned her torso towards him. "My due. I'm well aware Jock McIvor was a rich man. I've read all about the McIvor heiresses. They can't spend it all. Jock McIvor made it so hard for my mother to survive, she gave up on life. I'm not about to do the same. I want restitution for the sins of the past."

"You're nothing if not honest," said Adam.

"Isn't there a saying an honest lawyer is an oxymoron?" Casey shot back.

To his credit Adam laughed. "Touché. First Darcy and Courtney together with Curt and I as trustees would have to discuss the whole situation. Then we would suggest DNA testing. It could be arranged. It would take some time to get results of tests, say blood samples back. Tests would have to be sent to a lab in Brisbane."

"I'm in no hurry!" Casey answered promptly. "After all I've waited all my life." She looked across the table at Darcy, in some way deferring to her as did Courtney. "This is one magnificent homestead you've got here, Darcy. You could turn it into a hotel. I was wondering if I could stay a while before continuing on my way?"

Darcy stared back. This young woman who claimed to be their half sister had McIvor's riveting sapphire eyes with their bright look of challenge. But Darcy recognised suffering when she saw it. Casey was covering it well, but there was a haunting in their brilliant depths. "Whether you prove to be our half sister or not, Casey, you can stay," she said gently.

Casey smiled crookedly. "Tell you what, Darcy. You've got a heart."

At Adam's signal Courtney followed him out into the starry night on the pretext of reading the constellations in the desert sky.

"That's an extraordinary story Casey had to tell." Adam took her elbow as they walked down the short flight of steps to the home gardens. The palm of his hand only touched the point of her elbow, yet the thrill shocked her.

"You're not sure if you believe it?" Why would he? He had doubted her when she had returned to

Murraree at the bequest of her dying father. It was almost as though they were back to square one.

"Why do you say that?"

Her voice was ironic. "You're a very careful man."

"Courtney, I have to be. Ms McGuire on the surface appears to be who she says she is. But at this point we don't know. It has to be checked out."

She took a harsh breath. "Of course. But if what she's saying is true, while Mum was pregnant with me my womanising father was busy impregnating her mother."

"The story is far from new," he answered sardonically.

"Then who knows how many *more* might turn up?" Courtney burst out, then quickly bit her tongue.

Adam shrugged. "I have to admit it's a worry. The coverage of your father's death would have a lot to do with Casey's coming forward."

"I do wish they'd stop calling Darcy and me the McIvor heiresses." She made a little impatient gesture with her hand.

"Actually the label fits. You *are* heiresses."

"And we're so grateful we have you to look after us, Adam," Courtney spoke with exaggerated sweetness that stopped just short of anger. "I hid a smile when she took a crack at you. What was it? An honest lawyer is an oxymoron?"

"Heard it before," he said casually. "There are all kinds of jokes about lawyers. Here's one. Two lawyers were lost in the woods when they were confronted by a dangerous bear. One quickly removed his running shoes from his bag and put them on. The other stared at him. 'You can't outrun that bear.' The guy replied, 'I don't have to outrun the bear. I just have to outrun *you*.'"

Courtney laughed, but inside she was feeling decidedly on edge. Just when they were all settling down, an alleged long lost half sister turns up Adam's reaction, adding fuel to her ingrained wariness of him. "There's something very likeable about her, don't you think?" she questioned. "Something brave and strong. I can understand the rage in her heart about Dad and what happened to her mother. How very tragic. Casey is very confrontational. I suppose she'd have to be, given her sad life, but I can't help liking her. Darcy does, too."

"Maybe the answer is *blood*," Adam suggested. Casey McGuire was a very striking young woman but she wasn't his cup of tea. His cup of tea was a blue eyed blonde who didn't even come up to his shoulder. One, moreover, who didn't trust him. "I'd say she's a very tough, determined young woman. She could be hiding a lot."

"Like me?" Heat burned in her cheeks, making her feel glad of the star spangled darkness.

"No, not like you," he said.

"Goodness knows you were suspicious enough of me," Courtney continued as though he hadn't spoken. "For all I know you still are."

"You can't let that lie, can you?" He looked down at her halo of curls that managed to shine even at night.

"Sometimes I can, but now and again the memory peeks out. How you thought I unduly influenced Dad. The way you were ready to believe my ex-work mate's story of how I boasted I was going to twist a dying man around my little finger?"

"Ah, Courtney," he sighed. "The truth is whether you wanted to or not, you *did*."

Courtney tried hard to check her anger. After all, she had started this herself. "Typical lawyer's response. Now you have Casey's story to contend with. She covers up well but I think she's been dreadfully hurt."

"Which says a great deal for her survival skills. That's if her story's right," he cautioned. "If it is, there can be no doubt she's suffered. The nightmare of her mother's death and state homes aren't fun places. The question is did your father know of her mother's pregnancy? Did she contact him?"

"Maybe she felt she couldn't," Courtney, always tender-hearted, answered painfully. "Nobody there for her. Wanting to hide. She could have known he was married with a child. Who knows what he told her. Maybe he waited until she was entirely in his power before he told her and by then it was too late. He could even have told her he was single or let her assume he was. Casey didn't say."

"Casey was deliberately vague." Adam said, holding a palm frond up and away from her face. "Or she couldn't bear to speak about it. Your father could be ruthless but I don't think he would have abandoned Casey's mother because she was pregnant. He could have come to her aid in some shape or form. He could very easily have given her money to see her through."

"Maybe she didn't want money?" Courtney suggested, part of her thinking that might have been the answer. "She wanted *him*. She must have been madly in love with him. After all, she cut all her ties with her family for some kind of half life he promised her. She was young and she must have been a very vulnerable, needy person. Dad tired of her early."

"There's plenty of evidence that was his way," Adam said tonelessly.

"So it all started out very badly for Casey. She must have had an awful time at school. Born and raised in a little town where everyone knew everyone else's business. Her mother wasn't married and that carried a social stigma. No money. Then her extraordinary stand out looks. She's even taller than Darcy."

"But very female," Adam said dryly. "At this stage, Courtney, it would be a fatal mistake to swallow every word she's said. As remarkably as Casey resembles your father, such chance resemblances aren't unheard of. We've all seen people who could be someone else's double."

"Except she'd realise we would want proof?"

"Not necessarily." He led her towards a stone garden bench. "Women are notorious for plucking the heartstrings. Her story is just bad enough to earn her a lot of sympathy and possibly a reluctance to press her further."

"Well not sympathy from *you,*" she said sharply. "You have ice in your veins."

"I could change that opinion if you want."

She listened for derision. Heard none. Instead the sensual note in his voice caused a sudden flush of heat that coursed through her body. "I *don't* want, Adam. I don't want any complications."

A half smile lifted a corner of his chiselled mouth. "My sentiments as well, Courtney," he said suavely, pulling out a handkerchief and dusting off the area of bench where she intended to sit in her very pretty dress. "I wouldn't like it to be said I took advantage of an heiress. After all, it's what your father most feared."

Sweet smelling desert plants were flowering nearby. They filled the air with their fragrance. This area of the garden was secluded and still, full of shadows, with deep pockets of darkness. It was moonless but the stars were out in all their powerful brilliance, as beautiful as she had ever seen. Diamonds in a black-velvet sky. Beautiful, beautiful precious gems. She searched for the familiar clusters. Crux Australis, the Southern Cross, Triangulum Australe, the Southern Triangle, Corona Australis, the Southern Crown. They hung so low in the sky she felt like putting up a hand and pulling one down.

Catch a falling star. Make a wish.

What would it be? To find the man she wanted to share her life with? Was he already beside her? A cooling breeze had sprung up ruffling her hair. Little nocturnal creatures were scuttling about the garden. She felt all *sensation*. He made her that way. Presently to break the electric silence that had fallen between them she said, "My father showed compassion at the end, though, didn't he? He wanted to see me. He wanted to provide for me. I just can't go on believing there was no good in him. That he was totally without conscience or genuine feeling."

"Don't fret, Courtney." Gently he touched her shoulder. His arm had been leaning on the back of the bench behind her. "He wasn't. At the same time he turned the tables on Darcy who had devoted her life to him. Curt and I have become good friends. Curt makes no bones about the fact McIvor did everything in his power to keep Darcy tied to him and away from Curt, who's always loved her."

She felt guilty about that when she didn't need to feel guilty. "Now that I do believe. Darcy carried the burden, I know. I had a peaceful life with Mum. Lots of love and understanding. But Darcy was the one our father wanted. Not me. He would have crushed the life out of me. Just as he did my mother." Tears burned behind her eyes but she defied them to fall.

"I think not," Adam answered firmly, turning his dark head. "There's not much of you but I think you would have triumphed, Courtney. You have your own gutsy core."

"I'm not sure if that's a compliment or not." There was a faint edge to her voice.

"Why not?" His finger lightly brushed one of her bright curls. "Haven't I complimented you before?" He studied her enchanting profile.

He had kissed her, too. Rocking her to her foundations. "I'd better answer carefully, seeing you're a lawyer. I believe you told me I looked beautiful at the polo ball."

"Which you did. You wove magic. A trick women have."

"Trick?" She risked a glance at him. Saw the glitter of his eyes. "Sometimes I think a woman hurt you badly. A woman who looked a bit like me." What if he still loved that woman, Courtney thought. What *if?*

"Now you've caught me out," Adam said smoothly. "I was going for a time with a blue-eyed blonde. An associate in another law firm. She was very bright and very attractive, but nowhere near as lovely as you."

"So what happened?" His voice told her at one time this other girl had mattered.

"The usual thing. She cheated on me. I didn't like that. Especially as she'd already moved in with me. She swore it hadn't meant anything. A one night stand. She'd had a few drinks and one thing led to another. It was apparent she couldn't be trusted. Maybe if I'd really loved her I'd have been prepared to forgive her. As it was, we broke up."

"You mean *you* broke it up." She could just see him doing it. Clinical, dispassionate, shutting the door on his true feelings.

"Don't be so hard on me, Courtney," he groaned. "I take fidelity seriously. Don't you?"

"I've never actually lived with anyone," she said. "How long were you together?" It was very unsettling, these fierce stabs of jealousy.

"Pray tell, what is this?" He turned her face towards him, a finger on her chin. "Jealous?"

He was so mocking. *So* arrogant. "I'd prefer to say making conversation." Now her palm itched to hit him.

"Is that what it is?"

"Better to stick to conversation," she said.

"When a beautiful woman is born to be kissed?" He drew her to her feet and confounded her by rocking her gently in his arms. "It's been far too long, Courtney."

Had he spoken those exact lines to that other woman? Had he turned her heart upside down? Of course he had, he had perfected the art. Then he had left her. Was he telling the truth about that affair or just avoiding the real reason because he thought she would buy it? "If that's a prompt for a goodnight kiss, Adam, I'm sorry to disappoint you."

His dark voice mocked. "But you know you won't."

He didn't kiss her mouth at first, he kissed her eyelids. Then her cheek. Beneath her ear. She couldn't summon up the strength to stop him. She was already in too deep.

"Why did I wait so long?"

She didn't want him to wait. It was mad, perhaps ill advised, but she was wild for him.

His mouth found her own. His kiss, slow and very thorough. It robbed her of breath. She broke it with a little gasp but instead of releasing her he pulled her even closer, folding her petite body into his like a piece of origami. "You're interfering with my work, Ms McIvor," he said huskily.

"How is that?" Her own voice was ragged.

"It's hard to get a grip on a client's problem when you're thinking of someone else." He bent his head to her again. The tip of his tongue traced the outline of her tender mouth, then the soft inner cushion.

Her whole body, her entire network of nerves, was thrumming like high voltage electricity wires. "I can't believe you think of *me*, Adam?" She fought from going under. In too short a time Adam Maynard had gained a real hold on her. There was an inherent danger in that.

"Why is that?" He continued to taste her mouth and her skin as though they were ambrosial.

"A certain way you look at me hasn't changed." She voiced her deep concern.

That gave him pause. "Explain."

Tension began to vibrate like plucked strings. "The way we began. The lack of trust."

"We're not back to that," he groaned. "I was just trying to do my job, Courtney."

"Perhaps, but the fact is, the look's still there. It slips out from time to time. It distresses me."

Anger blazed up unexpectedly. "What else about me distresses you? Obviously not being in my arms. You let me kiss you like you couldn't live without it."

It was true. She opened up to him like a flower. But she wasn't *thinking*. She was *feeling*. "How do I know you're not on track to seduce me?" She had a sudden impulse to turn the tables. "It would be worth your while. I'm sure you make a lot of money as a full partner in your firm, but I'm an heiress, aren't I?" Immediately as she said it she was ashamed of the ploy. It was unworthy. A last ditch attempt to regain a little control. Adam wasn't a dishonourable man.

"Don't say any more, Courtney," he said tightly. "You've gone far enough." Never had a woman got to him so hard and fast. Never had a woman so insulted him.

It was a blow at his manhood. He hauled her back into his arms. Held her captive. This time the kiss *punished*.

Next morning Adam left on his journey back to Brisbane, leaving them both estranged.

It was 8:40 before Casey woke with brilliant sunlight streaming in from the verandah. For a few disoriented moments she couldn't think where she was. She'd never slept in such a beautiful room in her life. Never slept between crisp white sheets that puffed up an exquisite aroma as she moved. It wasn't any fragrance she knew. Not the usual lavender, gardenia or rose. She would have to ask what it was.

She swung her long legs out of the bed, curling her toes on the pale green carpet. The guest room had such a fresh airy feel. It had only just been re-decorated, she'd been told. The wallpaper was a wide cream and pale green stripe. The drapes a cream sheer that moved gently in the breeze. The circular bedside tables were covered in the same soft green, almost a lime. Taffeta decorated around the hem with silk tassels, matching the shades on the bedside lamps. The quilt and the scatter cushions introduced harmonious pinks and blues. Very good watercolours hung on the walls. There was a daybed, near the French doors and an upholstered bench at the end of the bed. A little writing table with a chair.

Casey picked up one of the various ornaments. A ballerina with legs almost as long as hers. She turned it over. Royal Copenhagen. It was all incredibly luxurious to Casey who had never experienced anything remotely like luxury in her life. The broken down old bungalow she'd grown up in leaked every time there was rain. And it *rained* in the tropics. The Home with the ghastly grey paint on the walls trimmed with black. Just the place for heart-sick kids. Next stop the streets or jail.

She'd had to fight for everything she wanted. She'd survived but she still had a lot of bad memories to clean out. Her mother hadn't survived, but she couldn't think of that now. She had to take a quick shower and go down for breakfast. Her half sisters weren't fools. They would want to know a lot more. They'd want proof. A sample of her DNA. Deoxyribonucleic acid. What a mouthful! She'd read somewhere the chemical that exists in all living organisms could survive in remains for thousands of years after death. So didn't that make the blueprint of life virtually indestructible? The name Jock McIvor hadn't appeared anywhere on her birth certificate. It had said Father: Unknown. But she was certain her DNA would find him out at long last. There had to be some justice in this world.

When she walked into the kitchen she found Courtney and her mother sitting talking quietly together, obviously close.

I don't belong here. I'm only passing through. Hang around a week or two. Settle on what's owed to me. Maybe I'll never belong anywhere.

Courtney saw her first, her small enchanting face lighting up in a smile. "Good morning, Casey. Sleep well?"

"Good morning, dear," Marian murmured politely, not allowing her blue eyes to remain on Casey very long. Marian found her remarkable resemblance to Jock just too painful.

"Slept like a log," Casey said. "Couldn't think where I was when I woke up. I've never slept in such a beautiful bedroom in my whole life. Correction. I've never slept in a beautiful bedroom period. The bed linen smells so fresh and lovely. What's it scented with?"

"Boronia," Courtney looked pleased Casey had noticed. "Our native boronia. It grows wild." She stood up with purpose, a petite figure in a pink tank top with white cotton jeans. "Now, what would you like for breakfast?"

Casey was so surprised she answered a little roughly, "You're not going to wait on me."

"No problem. Sit down. I've set a place. What do you usually have?"

Casey grimaced. "Cup of instant coffee. Couple of pieces of toast with honey. I'm usually on the run. I sing at night and do part-time jobs by day."

"You have a very distinctive speaking voice," Marian said, looking a bit strained. Marian found this tall young woman as intimidating in her way as McIvor had been in his.

"Don't tell me. Like Jock's?" Casey gave a brittle laugh, knowing the girls' mother hadn't really taken to her. Nor ever would.

"You might like some orange juice," Courtney intervened smoothly, setting a small glass before her. "Maybe a mango. We had a carton of them flown in from Bowen."

Casey shook her head, unsettling a couple of

long curling locks. This morning she didn't wear her hair loose. It was twisted into a high knot. "I've decided I could never eat another mango in my life," she confessed. "We had a tree in the backyard when I was a kid. It was loaded with fruit every year. Hundreds and hundreds of mangoes." She didn't say sometimes the fruit had kept them from starving. The mangoes, the pawpaws and the thousands of purple passionfruit. One couldn't really starve in the tropics. Then there was the Queensland nut tree, the macadamia and the thicket of avocados. She couldn't eat them, either. "The taste reminds me of…yesterday." The horrible years.

"Oh, Casey, that's so sad." Courtney had been watching Casey's eyes. "I tell you what I'm going to do. I'm going to make you some scrambled egg to go on your toast. How's that?"

"I don't *need* you to, Courtney." She spoke roughly again, trying to cover her embarrassment. The last thing she'd expected was to be welcomed and waited upon.

"Too bad because I want to." Courtney set to work.

"Where's Darcy?" Casey asked, realising little Courtney had a mind of her own.

"She's out. Running a station like this is a full-time job. I take care of all the domestic duties and most of the paper work, but I mean to get outdoors a lot more. Curt and Adam flew away early. Curt has a chain of stations to run. Sunset Downs is the flag-ship and the Berenger ancestral home. Adam had to get back to work in Brisbane. Peter is out exploring."

"I can't wait to," Casey said and laughed. "I've never been Outback in my life. It's another world. The space and the freedom. I adore it!" Why wouldn't she for that matter?

"Do you ride?" Marian asked, readily seeing this long legged young woman galloping off.

"You're joking!" Casey leaned across the table. "There's been no place for horse riding in my life. Back in the city it's an elitist past time. It costs money to buy a horse, and have it agisted in outer suburb acreage."

"You'll have to learn," Courtney said, sliding the pile of scrambled eggs onto a warmed dinner plate. "I couldn't ride, either. Not that I'm crash hot now, but Darcy taught me as much as she could. Darcy is a wonderful horsewoman. While you're here you have to have lessons."

"While I'm here?" Casey brushed a Titian curl away from her mouth. "What if I want to stay?"

"Would you *want* to stay if everything was set-tled?" Courtney asked in some surprise. "You know, when we have proof you're Dad's daughter?"

"Don't panic, Courtney." Casey picked up a fork. "That came off the top of my head. I've never set-tled anywhere for long. I'm just blowin' on the wind. But this is a great house. And so big! Who's going to live in it when Darcy moves away? She's getting married soon, isn't she?"

Courtney nodded. "The date's been set. May 24.'"

"So life moves on." Casey gave her a long considering look. "You and Darcy work like a team but half of the team will be gone. What about you? I read about your old job. Are you going to fly away?" Casey started to make inroads on the scrambled eggs. "Say, this is good!"

"I'm glad. I'll have to watch my diet all my life, I'm so small but you're like Darcy. You can eat."

"Because there's a lot more of us," Casey said, accepting piping hot toast. "It must have broken your hearts leaving Darcy behind," she said, lifting her eyes to study Marian's gentle face.

"You can't know, Casey," Marian said, unlike Courtney not seeing the sensitivity in the back of Casey's brilliant eyes.

"Oh, I think I can." Casey shrugged. "Sometimes I think I'd like to open my mouth and let it all pour out. What Jock McIvor did to my mother. The misery that descended on me. I've never got round to consulting anyone but I know I've got problems."

Marian tried to help. "A good counsellor trained in these matters could help you, Casey," she said.

"I'm not bad at helping myself," Casey said, fixing her eyes on Marian's face. "You had no idea about my mother?"

Marian visibly paled.

"Of course she didn't." Courtney sprang to her mother's defence.

"Almost from the beginning I suspected he had other women," Marian spoke falteringly. "Jock was a very physical man. He couldn't live without plenty of sex. I mustn't have been very good at it."

"Neither apparently was my mother," Casey said grimly. "He tired of her quickly. But then he didn't *love* women. He used them. Do you suppose, Marian—I'm asking you very seriously as a woman who might know—would my mother have contacted him about the pregnancy? Had you any inkling he was troubled?"

Marian sighed deeply. "Jock didn't talk to me, Casey. I was just decoration. I was as lovely as Courtney when I was young."

"Come on, you're still a very attractive woman," Casey replied. "Would you answer the question?"

"Jock was all sorts of things, Casey. He spent a lot of his life chasing women if they weren't actively chasing him but I don't believe he would have abandoned your mother. Or let her go it alone. After all, she might have borne him a *son*. A son would have been everything to Jock. I'm sure he'd have divorced me if your mother had given him a longed for male heir. Regardless of that, I'm certain had she contacted him he would have helped her, at the very least, financially."

"Not pressed for an abortion? She could have blackmailed him?"

"Jock knew your mother. The sort of young woman she was. He knew he was safe. On balance, Casey, I'd say your mother never found the courage to let him know she was pregnant. Jock was ruthless, but he wasn't entirely heartless."

Casey wasn't about to accept that. "If you'd seen my mother—she was petite like you and Courtney—you'd say he was pretty damned heartless. She cried oceans of tears. Then she started drinking. When cheap alcohol wasn't enough, she went on to drugs. People used to make fun of her. The kids at school were cruel."

"So you learned early to stand up for yourself?" Marian said.

"I'd like to tell you about the old battle-axe in The Home," Casey said, "but it would put me off my breakfast. I'd love a cup of coffee."

"Coffee coming up. You'll have one, Mum?"

Marian pushed back her chair and stood up. "No thank you, darling. I'll let you two talk. It's been a marvellous visit but Peter and I have to think about getting home."

* * *

"I trouble your mother, don't I?" Casey asked after Marian had left.

"A bit," Courtney was forced to admit. "Mum had to swallow a lot of humiliation in her time with Dad."

"I'm sorry I didn't meet up with him before he died," Casey said, her expression grim.

Courtney gave a strangled laugh. "He'd probably have left you the lot. No one ever knew what Dad planned to do."

"Sounds like he thought he was a king in his own kingdom."

Courtney was silent for a moment. "In lots of ways he was. It's different out here, Courtney. It's a man's world."

"And look what they've done with it." Casey grunted. "Where's home for Marian?"

"Brisbane. They have an apartment in Sydney as well. They often stay there. Peter owns a successful engineering business. Mum has been very happy with him."

"That's good." Casey nodded. "Sounds like she was unhappy for too long. Darcy seems to have landed herself the perfect man. Her fiancé is very impressive. What about the lawyer? Those black eyes of his don't miss a trick. You can bet your life he'll have me thoroughly checked out."

"As we speak." Courtney tried to keep the hostile note out of her voice.

"No love lost there?" Casey asked with sharp interest.

Courtney poured two cups of coffee, then sat down. "You must have researched our story thoroughly. When he was dying my father sent for me. I hadn't seen him since I was ten. For some convoluted reasons of his own, McIvor took a great fancy to me. It got so bad he seemed to prefer having me around than Darcy who had shown him nothing but loyalty and endless devotion. I know she was deeply hurt."

"Why the hell not!" Casey almost growled it. "You're saying it wasn't your fault?"

"Of course it wasn't!" Courtney's eyes flared. "I couldn't refuse to sit with him if he wanted me. He was dying. I think he was trying to make restitution. Adam didn't see it that way. He thought maybe I'd unduly influenced my father."

"Did you?" Courtney asked bluntly.

"Have you noticed how suspicious he is of *you?*" Courtney demanded to know. "You say you're on the level. So was I. I love Darcy. I couldn't do anything to hurt her."

"I can understand that," Casey said. "She struck me as a really good woman. As for you—" Casey gave her brilliant smile "—You're a darn good cook. Now there was something I was going to ask you. Do you remember a Troy Connellan? Maybe

I should be asking Darcy, seeing you haven't been back on Murraree long."

"Of course I know of the family," Courtney said. "Troy would be a couple of years older than Darcy. I actually don't remember him, but Darcy would know. Why do you ask?"

"Oh I met up with him in the town," Casey answered offhandedly. "Had dinner with him the night before I arrived. He invited himself. Big rugged guy. Full of himself like big rugged guys are. Now, what are we going to do today?" she asked. "Anything I can do to help? I'm good with machinery if something needs fixing." She fixed her eyes on Courtney's face. "You seem to have accepted me, Courtney. I could be an impostor."

"Not much chance of that." Courtney gave a brittle laugh. "You're just too much like Dad."

Casey wasn't kidding when she said she could fix machinery. Two of the mustering motor bikes needed a service. Casey took care of that, earning long admiring looks from the stockmen who rode them. Plenty of curiosity, too. Especially from the men who had seen Jock McIvor in his prime. Everyone knew there was a story about to unfold. Nothing surprising there considering McIvor's larger than life exploits. One of the best aboriginal horse whisperers whispered an aside to Courtney when she and Casey visited the yard. "*I* think Missy is who *she* thinks she is!"

"Don't tell anyone, Charlie, okay? We don't want it getting around."

"Got around already," Charlie said in a light ironic voice.

It was Curt who arranged for the DNA testing, by-passing the bush hospital at Koomera Crossing—there were far too many rumours flying—for the hospital at Alice Springs. There they learned it would be weeks before they would have the results. It didn't seem to matter. Casey had fitted in remarkably well, fixing things no one else seemed to know were broken.

They were walking down the main street, returning to their motel when they were hailed by a tall, rangy young man who flashed them all a wide smile. "Well what d'ya know! Long time no see. How are you, Curt?" He shot out his hand and Curt grabbed it, each clapping an arm around the other's shoulder.

"Just great, Troy! Have we missed you on the circuit! You've heard Darcy and I are engaged."

"Now why isn't that a surprise?" Troy Connellan turned to Darcy. "Hiya, Darcy. You're looking more beautiful than ever. Congratulations you two. You're meant for each other." He leaned forwards to kiss Darcy's uplifted cheek. "And this is? Don't tell me… She looks familiar but I can't place her."

"I'm the woman you had dinner with the other night," Casey flashed back.

"And you *didn't* ring me up. Shame on you," he said lazily. "We happened to meet up in Koomera Crossing," he explained to the others.

Darcy smiled. "So Casey told us."

"What did she say?" Troy asked with every appearance of eagerness.

"Nothing much," Casey said. "Only that you're full of yourself."

"Ms McGuire, whatever do you mean?"

"Look, why don't we all go some place and have lunch," Curt suggested, as tourists to the Centre flowed around them. "We're flying back this afternoon. Courtney stayed at home so Darcy wants to get back."

"Ah, yes, Courtney. It must be great to have your sister back in your life, Darcy?" Troy gave her an understanding look.

"It is, Troy," she said quietly. "It's wonderful."

"And this red-haired woman here?" Troy looked down from his superior height on Casey. "Pardon my asking, but would she be one of Jock's?"

Knowing Troy for all of his life Curt wasn't surprised by the audacity of the question. "That we have to find out," he answered easily.

"Yeah, well, she'd sure pass for one." Troy Connellan grinned. "Told me the other night she'd come Outback to find you, Darcy. Seems she has."

"Which is why we're anxious to find out if there is a relationship," Darcy said. "We already know one thing for certain, Casey is an asset around the place."

"Excuse me? You're telling me you can ride a horse, Casey?"

"Darcy means I'm pretty good at fixing things."

"Really? Like what for instance?"

"Are you any good at anything else but heckling?" Casey asked.

"Break it up you two." Curt looked from one to the other with interest.

"Just a bit of sparring," Casey said, putting out a hand and giving Connellan a good hard thump on the back.

"So what are you doing at The Alice, Troy?" Curt asked when they were seated at a restaurant table. "Business?"

Troy Connellan leaned back, his smiling face abruptly sobering. "I'm taking a few days off trying to figure out what I'm going to do with the rest of my life."

"Oh, Troy!" Darcy all but wailed.

"Hang in there," Curt advised firmly. "Vulcan is your birth right. It will come to you."

"Maybe." Troy's golden eyes narrowed. "Dad could pass it on to Leah. He's threatened me that's what he's going to do."

"He's just cracking the whip," Darcy said, reaching out to give Troy's hand a pat. "Everyone knows how much your father depends on you whether he says so or not. Leah spends most of her time in Sydney living it up."

"Only thing, Dad's a whole lot fonder of her than of me," Troy said dryly. "Anyway don't let's worry about it now. Let's enjoy ourselves. I can't tell you how glad I am you and Curt have finally got together. I think my Dad is pretty bad, but McIvor was a regular *bastard!*"

Amen, thought Casey. Even Darcy didn't look defensive on her father's account. Connellan, Casey figured was as outspoken as she was. And what was with his father? Who was Leah? Casey found she actually wanted to know but the subject had been dropped.

Lunch consisted of a huge platter of Gulf crab, wok fired peppery squid, crisp fried prawns and baby barramundi in a beer batter served with fresh lemon wedges, accompanied by individual servings of a tangy Thai salad. The lot washed down with an ice cold beer. Outside the air-conditioned restaurant the pavements were scorching.

No one wanted dessert. They didn't need it after that.

"Why don't you stay on a couple of days and see something of the Centre now you're here?" Troy suggested, looking at Casey. "I'm a free man for a coupla days. I could show you around. There's Uluru and the Olgas, Kata Tjuta about 50 K's west. Rainbow Valley has to be one of *the* beauty spots in the Outback. I love it. The colours are extraordinary. What do you say?"

Blasé Casey was so dumbfounded she couldn't hide her surprised expression. "I say, no. For one I don't have any clothes. I already know *you're* nuts. And I don't have money to throw around."

"You don't need it," Troy said. "Do like you do back in Brissie. Sing for your supper. Have you heard this girl sing and play guitar?" Troy shot an enquiring look at Curt and Darcy who were sitting back holding hands. "I mean, she's just beautiful. When she *sings*," he joked. "I've never heard anyone as good before and there are a few around. Also she plays a mean guitar."

Darcy's lovely smile broke out. "That's a pleasure we can look forwards to. Why *don't* you stay, Casey. We can vouch for Troy. Generally speaking he behaves himself. You can buy a few things in town to tide you over. Curt can fix it for your accommodation, can't you, Curt?"

"Easily," he said. "It's not such a bad idea, Casey. You want to see the real Outback."

"Not with this guy I don't."

"It's not like that at all," Troy grinned. "Underneath she really likes me."

Which she did. But Casey, who had handled a lifetime of deprivation couldn't handle kindness and friendship. "No really, let's forget about it." She was starting to feel overwhelmed.

Darcy shook her gleaming dark head. "Not when we can see you want to stay. It's only for a couple of days anyway."

Kindness and generosity seemed to emanate from Darcy. *Her big sister?* "I promised Courtney I'd—"

"Whatever it is it'll keep," Darcy said firmly as though she were there for the express purpose of working things out. "Courtney would urge you to stay and see the sights. It's the perfect opportunity."

I'm not really ready for this, Casey thought. It's too hard to take. I was ready for hostility, anger, bitter resentment, even blame. Instead it was like they all knew she was going to turn up one day. "You're too nice to me," she said abruptly, thinking the milk of human kindness had rarely been allotted to her.

"Who could deny a *goddess!*" Troy pressed back in his chair, smiling his bold tantalising smile.

"It's settled then," Darcy said, eyes sparkling. "Give us a call when you want to come home."

Never had Casey been so glad she had her sunglasses on. She who never cried except on increasingly rare occasions when she was flooded by her nightmares, felt the sting of tears in her eyes.

Home? Did she have a home? If she hadn't been such an undemonstrative person she would have put her arms around Darcy and hugged her.

CHAPTER THREE

TROY CONNELLAN didn't waste any time. He had a tour of the Olgas, Kata Tjuta lined up by midafternoon.

"I wanted you to see Kata Tjuta first," he told her, covering the distance from the Alice to the ancient domes in record time. His late model, top of the range 4WD was air-conditioned which Casey privately found heavenly after the ute.

"Why's that?" Just looking out at the extraordinary landscape was an inspiration for endless songs.

"I'd better whisper this," he laughed, "but I find the Olgas even more alluring than Uluru. They're completely different from the Rock. Almost like male and female. I wanted you to note the contrast."

"You're being real nice to me, Troy." Deliberately she used an exaggerated drawl. "But it won't get you *nowhere*."

"Is that all you think about?" He gave her a gleaming sarcastic look. "Sex?"

"Hell, I was talking about singing," she lied. "Sex is out of the question."

"You mean you won't be moving into my room?"

"Nope. You're too young for me. Do you like Darcy?"

"Sure do," he said. "Darcy is a lovely woman. Curt is my good friend. They'd have been married years ago only for McIvor."

"So you as good as told us," Casey said dryly, still staring through the window. She was thrilled by the wonder of the Outback bird life. It was so prolific! The great flights of budgerigar were amazing! The gold and green of Australia, the gold and green of the wattle, flying in formation swooping then soaring for all the world like a trained aerobatics team. "Darcy has been remarkably accepting of me despite the fact she has no actual proof. So for that matter have Courtney and her mother, who by rights should hate me."

"Why should anyone hate you?" He swung his golden-brown head sharply. "You were the innocent victim."

She shrugged. "My mother stole McIvor away. At least for a little while."

"She paid dearly for the association," Troy pointed out grimly. "For what it's worth, Casey, if you *are* Jock McIvor's daughter and I can't see who else you might be, I don't think he turned his back on your mother knowing she was pregnant. The man was a tyrant walking all over everyone but he wasn't that bad."

"Why didn't he contact her to find out if she was okay?" she demanded to know. "No, he did nothing of the kind. He gave way to his lust and moved on. I despise him."

"Pretty awful to have so little respect for one's father."

"Are you talking about mine or yours?" she retorted sharply.

He winced. "I can't hide the fact my dad and I don't get on."

"Darcy and Curt seem to worry about you?"

"They know the full story, Casey. We all grew up together."

"So what *is* the full story?" She wanted a full run down.

His powerful sex appeal fairly crackled. "Oh, I'll tell you one time when we're tucked up in bed together."

"Just as I thought," she groaned. "You arranged this so we could wrestle the night away having wild sex?"

"You're reading my mind," he laughed. "No, Casey, you're safe with me. I haven't forgotten that snap kick or the hook to the jaw. I didn't tell you but it was sore for days."

"Good," she said heartlessly.

"How blunt you are," he said. "I like that in a woman."

Talk was impossible as the fantastic weathered domes of Kata Tjuta loomed up, getting bigger and bigger as they approached.

"Glory Be!" Casey muttered in awe.

The prehistoric domes rose to maybe a couple of thousand feet from the completely flat surrounding plain. She tried to count them. Gave up.

"More than fifty," Troy said, reading her mind. "The explorer Ernest Giles described them as 'rounded minarets, giant cupolas and monstrous domes.' They're considerably higher than the Rock. The two principal domes Ghee and Walpa are dedicated to Wanambi, the great Rainbow Serpent of the Dreaming. Kata Tjuta means many heads in Pitjantjatjara. That's a tribe of the Centre. Tourists are forbidden to visit after dark."

"I can understand that." Casey, who had proved herself brave in the line of fire, confessed, "It's kinda scary."

"All the ancient monuments are," Troy confirmed. "At certain times they have a very real aura of foreboding. I've felt it enough to have the hairs on the back of my neck stand on end. We have an equivalent of the Yeti around here as well. Pungalunga Men. They were giant cannibal gods who turned up at the time of the Dreaming. They raped the women and hunted down the aboriginal men with tjunas, hunting sticks. Then they ate the lot. You wouldn't want to meet up with one."

"And he mightn't want to meet up with me," Casey said. "Well not lately. I can't wait to get out and look around. I'm awfully glad you suggested this trip—whatever your ulterior motive—and Darcy talked me into it." Darcy had even accompanied her on a quick tour of the shops where she bought a few necessary things which included a couple of new cap sleeve T-shirts and the black sand blast denim shorts she was wearing right now.

"What do they remind you of?" Troy asked as they stood out on the red ochre plain dodging the ubiquitous Spinifex and clumps of other sharp edged grasses.

She turned to him, her expression so radiant, so transformed, he took a jerky breath. Tough as he was Troy was a romantic at heart. This woman, prickly as the Spinifex, looked glorious. Even dressed the way she was. Creak Akubra pulled down over her face, blazing eyes in shadow. Her white T-shirt, printed all over in blue, had tiny sleeves that showed off her slender arms and her beautiful high breasts. Her long legs unveiled of her jeans fell into the Wow category, not the luminous porcelain of her face but lightly tanned. Maybe she nearly topped six feet but boy, was she elegant. Grace in motion. An attribute she shared with Darcy. If she ever wanted to quit singing she could easily become a top model. Her magnificent torrent of hair fell in a thick pony tail down her back. On her feet she wore black slip-on sneakers. He cursed himself now for not buying a camera. He had a number of cameras but they were back on Vulcan.

"So what are you staring at, Connellan?" she asked, her voice full of challenge.

"I was just thinking how tall you are," he answered lazily.

"Bastard," she snapped.

"Now, now, language!"

She strode ahead. "Little did I know when I was born how tall I was going to be," she said when he caught up with her.

"Seriously, Casey, I like it. It's so nice to meet a woman face-to-face. Anyway, you're not as tall as me."

"That's good to know."

"What I was really thinking was you look gorgeous."

"Tell 'em anything," she scoffed. "Is that your way with women?"

"I don't have a way with women, no matter what they tell me. You *are* a very beautiful woman."

"When I'm sitting down, you mean." She shrugged off the compliment.

"You're not seriously hung up on your height, are you?" he asked, studying her profile with that cool little dimple in her chin.

"When I was a kid in The Home, when I wasn't praying to just die like my mum, or have some maniac off the streets run in and shoot me, I prayed I wouldn't grow any taller. Needless to say that fella up there—" she rolled her eyes skywards "—didn't hear me."

"Hell, Casey!" He felt like grabbing her, rocking her back and forth like a child needing comfort. "That's sad."

She laughed. "Not really. My height and my long legs came in handy. Now Courtney is a dainty little darling… You haven't seen her yet. She's quite lovely."

"She had curls like Shirley Temple when she was a kid."

Casey grunted. "We had a bitch of a matron at The Home—looked like a deranged orangutan— who cut all my hair off when I moved in. Said I had nits. I didn't. Red hair offended her. So did curls. Say, will you look at the colour of this soil! I mean really, are we on Mars?"

"I know what you mean but we're smack bang in the Wild Heart."

"And it's wonderful beyond words!" Impulsively she threw up her arms to the peacock-blue sky. "You asked me what the domes remind me of. They're changing all the time, even the colours are changing, but my first thought was they're all that's left of some very ancient civilisation. Long before the Pyramids and the ancient city of the Incas. The domes lean together for support as though eons ago some great shift in the earth's crust almost sent them tumbling. They have to be one of the great sights of the world surely?"

"Jewels of the desert," Troy said. "Like the Rock they go through numerous colour changes. Now they glow like red-hot coals. Later they'll cool off to pink and salmon. Towards dusk they're a lovely bluish-purple. Under clouds they're an eerie silver-grey. There are a lot of legends attached to Kata Tjuta but they're secret, known only to the aboriginal people."

They stayed until dusk, driving the full circle of the desert monuments a distance of some thirty kilometres, then wandering through the great ravines where that day only a fresh, gentle breeze was blowing.

"It's not like this all the time," Troy said, loping like a top athlete beside her. "At other times a howling wind makes the gorges a frightening place to be caught. An area at the north eastern end is rightly named the Valley of the Winds."

"It's marvellous," Casey said, her vivid imagination captured and held. As a child in The Home she had checked out lots of beautiful places in the scant library so she could transport herself there at night. She had sailed the Great Barrier Reef long years before she managed to land a gig on one of the islands. She had stood before the Great Pyramid of Giza, the Parthenon in Greece, the Colosseum in Rome, Saint Peter's. She had been on safari in Africa, visited Abraham Lincoln's monument, peered through the gates of Buckingham Palace though she never did manage to see the Queen, walked every inch of the Champs Elysees, stood beneath the great stone arch of the Arc de Triomphe. Even in that terrible place for frightened and abused children her imagination had flowed freely. It had probably saved her sanity.

A few minutes after Troy spoke the breeze suddenly lifted. It flapped at their clothes, causing them to cram their Akubras more firmly on their heads. The next moment without warning a huge bird—it was a wedge tailed eagle—took off from way above them causing a mini-landslide of fairly solid stones from the cracks and crevices.

Troy's arm shot out. His powerful hand clamped around Casey, pulling her back to safety, pinning her with his hips. She threw her arms out wide against the great granite wall, her back to him as he pressed her to it.

"Heck that was close!" he laughed, his clean breath warm against the side of her face. "You okay?"

"Sure!" she answered a little hoarsely. In truth the intimacy of the moment shocked her. And she didn't shock easily. Blood rushed through her body, speeding from her face to her feet. She liked this guy too much. He was getting to her. That in itself was threatening.

"Well are you going to come away from that wall?" Laughter again, stirring the skin of her nape.

Her cheeks smarted. She spun, so close to him she could see the fine grain of his tanned polished skin, the thickness of his eyelashes, the clarity of his eyes. "You clamped me so tight I was practically eating volcanic rock."

"Ungrateful woman!" He dusted his hands of grit. "Okay, we better get going. The wind's rising."

When finally they drove away the magical domes stood sharply silhouetted against a larkspur sky.

"Uluru tomorrow," Troy promised her. "The difference to me is the difference between the magical and the sublime. Uluru *is* Australia."

That evening she wore her other new T-shirt with her jeans and one of her favourite belts with the big oval buckle studded with red, white and blue rhinestones. The T-shirt was a cap-sleeve white polo with a deep V-neck and a small logo printed in red. Her afternoon in the desert had consumed her. How could you put an experience like that to music? And that wasn't the only insight she had gained. Troy Connellan had left his mark on her. At some elemental level he felt familiar to her and she didn't know why. He didn't seem like a near stranger at all. Maybe she had known him in another life. Slept with him. Sensation rippled over her when she thought of their close encounter. Her butt rammed into his crotch so she felt his unmistakable arousal. His heart beat striking chords in her breasts. For a few staggering moments she'd been so turned on she couldn't shift her position. Which he had mocked. The all-conquering male. God's gift to women. No way was he going to get under her guard again.

No way!

Midmorning found them joining a group of tourists as they were being shown around the rock by one of the aboriginal elders. Troy must have known him because they exchanged waves before he and Casey broke away so they could observe the mighty monolith on their own.

Casey was in two minds as to which of the great desert monuments she thought the most spectacular. In the end she came down on the side of Uluru because of its tremendous aura. Nothing fanciful; very slightly grotesque as with the Olgas, Uluru was a masterpiece of *oneness*. An island mountain of immense size, the largest rock in the world. Its enormous red dome totally dominated the vast empty landscape of Spinifex and sand.

"Well?" Troy asked. He'd been deriving great pleasure from her spontaneous reactions to the Heartland. Her changes of expressions were fascinating. Here was a woman who prized *freedom*.

"It's nearly impossible to say," she announced slowly. "Both great monuments strike awe into the heart but there's something so strong, so enduring, so mystical about the Rock. This has been a marvellous experience for me."

"Well you are looking at one of the great natural wonders of the world. To the aboriginal people Uluru is sacred."

"I'm not surprised. I think you came up with the right word for the Rock. Sublime. Does it go through all the colour changes like Kata Tjuta?"

"Absolutely. The spectacular colour changes are the most famous characteristic of all the desert monuments. The full range is quite remarkable from dawn when the sun touches the crest of the dome and it starts to glow the most beautiful golden-red. As the sun travels higher the colour begins to intensify until it's the brilliant orange-red it is now.'

"Have you ever climbed it?" she asked, aware of recent times the aboriginal custodians took a dim view of tourists clambering all over their sacred site.

He nodded. "It's a formidable climb, you know."

"It looks it." Casey's eyes rose to the summit.

"I first climbed it when I was fourteen with my dad. Then again when I was around eighteen with a friend. I won't be climbing it again. The tribal elders have made it known they don't like people walking all over it."

"Fair enough," Casey said. "It *looks* sacred."

Troy nodded. "Having said that, the view from the top is magnificent. Unforgettable. One of the times when the Rock looks its most beautiful is after the rains when it's surrounded by a sea of sparkling green water that's surprisingly cold. Beautiful waterfalls tumble down the many ravines and numerous crystal clear rock pools are formed. Of course the water disappears fairly quickly but it leaves in its wake a verdant belt all around the base. The wildlife love it. There are other amazing places I can show you if you stick around. Kings Canyon. Rainbow Valley. Mount Connor about 100 K's east. That's another island mountain with a majestic table top. The Devil's Marbles about 400 K's north of Alice. Palm Valley which is quite staggering in the middle of the arid desert—Chambers Pillar the last vestige of an ancient plateau. They're all wonderful."

"You love this part of the country, don't you?"

He smiled, his eyes a tawny gold. "My home is my favourite place in all the world."

"Have you seen much of the world?" Why not? He'd been born with a solid gold spoon in his mouth.

Just as she expected, he nodded, but casually. "I and a friend of mine from University—the same friend who climbed the Rock with me—took a year off so we could take the grand tour. We had a wonderful time. The world we live in is truly marvellous. I soaked up everything I saw, but my heart's here in the Outback. I'm very proud I'm Australian."

"But you don't think your father is going to leave you what you consider is your inheritance?" she prodded, her eyes on his firm but oddly voluptuous mouth. It was generous, curvy, so, so inviting. It made her want to… She reined herself in hard.

The gleaming eyes burned. "He cracks the whip from time to time thinking he can keep me in line."

"You'd think he'd revel in having a son?" Casey said, aware McIvor had been very bitter about the fact he had no male heir.

"It's like I said, Casey. My dad and I don't get on."

"Is Leah your mother, sister, sister-in-law, Dad's mistress?" No one had told her like it was some big secret.

He went to say something. Thought better of it. "Leah is my sister. She's broken all the rules for years and years but she could get away with murder as far as Dad's concerned. He spoils her like you wouldn't believe. But for some reason he's been very demanding with me."

"He expects more of you obviously."

"I don't know that I have that much more to give," he confessed wryly. "I've led a pretty tough solitary life of late up in the Territory. It's my job to oversee the chain and keep everyone in line."

"It's as well you're a great big fella. And your mother? What's she like?"

His face was turned to her so for a split second she was witness to the grief in his eyes. In a blink it was gone. "My mother's dead, Casey," he said, flatly.

"I'm sorry. How old were you?" For a minute she thought he wasn't about to answer.

"Fourteen. It wasn't all that long after I climbed the Rock, oddly enough. She and a family friend were caught in a flash flood on the station. You wouldn't realize it in a million years how quickly a near dry water channel can turn into a raging torrent unless you've seen it happen. It was a freak thing. They couldn't have been paying enough attention. They weren't prepared." He made a gesture with his strong brown hand as though warding the memory off.

"How dreadful." She was sure he wasn't telling her everything but she knew better than to pry. "I was eleven when my mother died," she offered out of some sort of fellow feeling. "She OD'd on drugs. She was thirty-six. A tiny little person. When I came home from school I thought she was asleep. She used to sleep for hours on end. I called the ambulance but I knew she was already dead."

"God Almighty!" Troy said quietly. "That must have ripped you apart?"

She kept staring at the magnificent desert monolith drawing on its strength. "These days, Connellan, I do my best not to let the memories in. I'd say just like you."

"Did you have anyone to talk to?"

"Oh sure," she said laconically. "I did a lot of talking to myself. No one else wanted to know. No aunts, no uncles, no cousins. Certainly no father. There was one compassionate lady who I think wanted to adopt me, but she was cut out of the frame. Almost immediately I was put in a home. The Home I call it. It was practically unendurable. Full of demons." She turned to him. Begged. "Please shut me up."

"No, let it out," he said from a great reservoir of compassion. "Though I can't talk, I see the importance of bringing things out into the open, but I can't seem to do it. The only trouble is bad memories reverberate down the years."

"You can say that again." Casey shuddered. "After I lost my mother it was like I had nothing and no one. I was nothing. You can see why I hate McIvor?"

Troy was shaking his head. "I'm certain he didn't know about *you*, Casey."

Her sapphire gaze turned stony. "He could have prevented a tragedy. My mother was a very vulnerable person. She couldn't come to terms with abandonment. She needed a man in her life. Not any man. McIvor. She was very pretty before she let herself go. She could have found a decent man but she was totally one track. Sometimes I think my mother and I came from a totally different species. I saw little kids like her in The Home. It chewed them up and spat them out."

"When did you leave?" he asked, really wanting to know.

"The grand old age of sixteen. No *sweet* sixteen, though somehow I emerged a virgin if you're interested in trivia."

A look of anger swept his face. "Casey, couldn't you have spoken to someone?"

She shrugged as though it were all too much in the past. "The place was full of creeps and monsters. There was one guy I called the Cobra—for obvious reasons—he was always set to strike. He had a greasy medusa of dreadlocks that stank. He was always trying to grab me. My heart used to beat like a drum at a military tattoo whenever he was around. He nearly scored one time—I was pinned to the mat—but I managed to get in an almighty kick that settled him very nicely. It certainly wasn't my pitiful cries of *Help! Help! Somebody help me!* that did it. He didn't come back for more. In fact, I didn't have a lot of trouble with anyone after that."

"And that was?" Troy questioned.

"When I was fourteen. So we both had terrible struggles at the same age. Now why have I told you all this?" she asked, frowning. "I don't talk about any of this stuff."

"Maybe it's the timelessness of our surrounding," he suggested very seriously. "The peace and the power. You're safe here. Safe from all the suffering of the past."

His eyes held her, full of fire, intelligence, understanding, more compassion than she had ever seen. It reminded her just how much she was falling under his spell.

"Only one thing. I can't set up a tent here." She veered off to joking. "Hard to nip out for a loaf of bread and a bottle of milk."

He smiled, stood up and extended a hand. "Let's

walk. The caves around the base of the Rock are shrines for the aborigines. Hundred of rock paintings decorate the walls. Uluru is *holy*."

Maybe some of that holiness will rub off on me, Casey prayed.

Like the night before they had dinner together. Nothing elaborate. Grilled fillet of prime beef with a horseradish sauce and a rocket salad on the side.

"That was good!" Casey said, "I've never tasted such flavoursome tender beef in my life."

"Well if you can't get it here you can't get it anywhere," Troy said, a smile on his curvy mouth.

"Dessert?"

"I think not. Maybe a short black then I intend taking a walk before turning in. The stars out here have to be seen to be believed."

"No pollution," Troy explained, topping up her wineglass with the last of the shiraz they had shared.

"You can't think a couple of glasses of wine will make me tipsy?" she mocked.

"No. Absolutely not," he replied dryly. "Making love to disoriented women isn't my scene."

She stared back at him wondering if he were joking. "Do you want to add anything to that?" she asked. "Like you're hoping, damned well *expecting* you're going to make love to me?" Suspicion was built into her.

"Isn't making love the most wonderful thing in the world?" His golden gaze was fixed on her, brilliant, unblinking. Just like a big cat.

"Try bungee jumping," she said. "Now that's a *real* thrill."

"You've done it?" Intensity turned to considerable interest.

"Sure have." Casey shrugged. "Had the time of my life. Beats sex hands down."

"So what say we go bungee jumping together?" he suggested, his mouth curling.

"Maybe. I promise you you'll be back for more."

"You're some woman, McGuire," he said, holding up a hand to signal the waitress.

Afterwards they took a stroll beneath the desert sky. He with the easy graceful lope she had come to admire. He looked like he had all the time in the world to get anywhere. Scorching hot during the day, the desert cooled off to a surprising degree at night. The air was crisp but as soft as silk. The desert scents subtle but wonderfully aromatic. Maybe it was the wine but her body felt warm, darn near hot. The memory of that incident at Kata Tjuta had stayed with her. The sexual intimacy. Never mind his response, it was hers she was worried about. Even so she knew Troy Connellan wasn't the kind of guy who would pounce on her for all his resemblance to a big tawny cat. She had more than enough experience to pick the bad guys. But she had to face the fact he was pushing her sexual buttons with no trouble at all.

Above them the stars were blazing. There was only a horned moon. The stars were unbelievably beautiful, dominating the vast sky.

"This is enthralling!" She blew out a little breath, wondering if being in the Outback was the source of a new-found inner serenity. The Outback was so vast. So open. So free. Incomparable Nature, the great healer.

"There are innumerable aboriginal myths about the sun, the moon and the stars," Troy was saying with that seductive edge to his voice. It was inbuilt, she'd noticed, not assumed. "The desert tribes know practically every star in the heavens. They all have a story."

"Do you know any?" she asked, lifting a hand to her loose blazing hair.

"Of course I do," he scoffed. "This is *my* country."

"So tell me. I love stories. I used to make up tons of stories to comfort myself when I was a child."

"Did you?" His eyes burned brighter than the stars. "Well there's the one about the Moon and the Morning Star. Our magnificent waterlily—you've seen them crowding the lagoons at Murraree—is the aboriginal symbol for a star. The flower is its beautiful luminous glow. The stalk is the star's path across the sky. We have a magnificent bark painting of the Morning Star back on Vulcan. I'll show it to you one day. It's mine and no one else's. My mother left it to me. She's up there, you know, in the Milky Way?" He lifted his heavy handsome head to the diamond river in the sky.

"That's lovely!" Casey breathed, for once without her trademark tinge of sarcasm. "So's mine."

"So we're friends, McGuire." He turned to her, holding out his large strong hand.

"Friends." Almost solemnly they shook hands. "Now tell me the story," she said, needing to downplay the emotion of the moment.

She hadn't meant him to kiss her when he showed her to her door. She opened her mouth to say good night, but he drew her fully, completely, into his arms, breast to breast, hip to hip, long legs near matched. Wave after wave of steamy sensation flowed down Casey's spine. She'd known from the beginning he could kiss like this.

He didn't hold back. Neither did she. This was something she wasn't going to think about. She was going to *take*. When the kiss broke, they were both breathing hard.

"Nice going, Connellan," she managed to gasp, starkly aware she wanted him with a force that shocked her.

"I want that to last until the next time I see you," he said huskily, slowly sliding his hands down her bare arms. He half turned towards his room at the end of the hallway. "Sleep tight, Red. Your mouth has the taste of sugar and spice. I have to tell you I just loved it on my tongue."

CHAPTER FOUR

SOMEONE of influence must have speeded up the DNA report because it came back less than a fortnight later. Casey was indeed who she said she was: Jock McIvor's daughter.

The only one who was shocked was Casey herself. On receiving confirmation, she tore down the front steps of the homestead where the three McIvor women had been relaxing over coffee, and out into the scorching noonday sun heading for the station jeep, mercifully parked in the shade.

"Oh, she's terribly upset!" Tender-hearted Courtney clutched her throat. "We should go after her."

"No, let her be." Darcy put out a restraining hand. "She has to be on her own for a while. It's asking too much of her not to be upset. All her life Casey hasn't known who her father was. She's only learned that fairly recently. It's a lot to take in. In a weird way Casey, too, had to have proof positive.

I'm so glad Adam is coming this weekend," she breathed. "We have to sort out Casey's fair share."

"That's okay with me," Courtney readily agreed. "Casey's not one to confide, but I'd say she's had a pretty awful life. Plenty of hard knocks."

"God alone knows what happened at that orphanage." Darcy grimaced. "And finding her mother like that! What can one say? It makes our stories pale into insignificance."

"Do you really suppose Dad didn't know?" Courtney searched her sister's crystal clear eyes.

Darcy turned her considering gaze to the home gardens, shimmering in the golden heat. "I couldn't bear to think he abandoned a pregnant woman. I couldn't cope with that. Then again that's not being fair to Dad. I knew him as well as anyone. I'm certain he had no idea."

"Surely he could have checked?"

"I suppose he relied on the woman protecting herself. Casey's mother should have contacted him. I'd say she didn't feel able. She must have been a young woman with lots of problems. She didn't contact her parents, either. Not even for Casey's sake. She must have come to believe herself an outsider. I can't think much of her parents not searching for her. It's a sad story, but we have to care for Casey now. She's our sister. We won't do the half sister bit."

"Sister is better," Courtney agreed. "So why

don't we turn the news into a little celebration? Nothing Casey would find hard to handle. She's not used to being fussed over."

"What do you have in mind? A few people over for the weekend?"

"Exactly." Courtney smiled. "Troy Connellan for one now he's back. I think Casey really likes him even if she won't let on."

"Leah's home." Darcy frowned, like that was a problem. "We can't avoid inviting her. She's probably got some guy in tow."

"You're the one who knows her," Courtney said. "We only met up that once in town. She struck me as very, very snobby."

"And no one would know what about. She's not a bit like Troy, and her father has spoilt her rotten. Yes, a nice weekend shared with friends might well be what we need. Nothing that will drive Casey away. I want her to enjoy it."

"I don't imagine anyone will be surprised she's Dad's daughter?" Courtney asked, beginning to stack the cups and saucers.

"No," Darcy answered simply. "Not when Dad spent years enrapturing women."

"What would we do if someone else turns up?" Courtney paused in what she was doing.

"Interesting question," Darcy sighed. "They'd have to do like Casey. Prove themselves. One thing's certain. If Dad has a *son* we can be absolutely certain he knew nothing about it. I spent years feeling guilty I didn't have a penis. Besides I don't believe his gold digging girlfriends wouldn't have told him. So that's one issue out of the way. As for Casey? I don't want her to disappear out of our lives, do you?"

"Oh, no!" Courtney shook her head. "She's our blood. Why, do you think she will? After things are settled I mean."

"She could." Darcy sighed. "She has her own life. She's very talented. And she's knock your eyes out stunning. Surely that's a winning combination in show business. But Casey has fitted right in. She seems to love it here. Her personality is unfurling like a flower to the sun. She has a wicked sense of humour. She makes us laugh. We love to hear her sing. She's so good. She pours her heart into everything. And she writes her own material. Add to that, she's very supportive and so effective around the place."

"I'll say!" Courtney agreed with a wry shrug. "Sometimes she makes me feel a touch inadequate."

"Don't be silly!" Darcy looked at her younger sister, sharply alerted by some tentative note in her voice. "We all have our strengths. You're the brains of the outfit."

"Now *you're* being silly." Courtney smiled, at the same time feeling reassured.

"You know what I mean. I rely on you to keep the homestead running smoothly. As far as the business side goes you've been a great asset. We're a team. A team I'd like Casey to join if she ever wanted to."

"Well she looks to you more than me," Courtney admitted freely. "When she first arrived she reminded me of a boxer forever dancing on his toes. Now she's learning to relax around us."

"She's family," Darcy said.

Courtney didn't delay inviting the weekend guests. At first Casey looked doubtful. She didn't want to be put into the position of guest of honour but Darcy assured her there simply wasn't going to be any fuss. They were all going to enjoy themselves. What was more Casey's status as Jock McIvor's daughter would be confirmed. No family conflicts. All the gossipmongers could forget about that. Casey McGuire-McIvor had been readily accepted by her sisters.

"So do I know anyone who's coming outside of Curt and Adam?" Casey asked, wariness in her sapphire eyes.

"We invited Troy Connellan. You know him." Courtney kept her tone casual. "His sister Leah is at home so we've invited her and her current boyfriend. You'll like our other guests. They're very easygoing people. All pastoral families. Twelve in all. Just the right cosy number. What was the point of restoring the homestead if we can't have friends over?"

"So what is it I'm not going to like about Troy's sister?" The ever sharp Casey asked.

"I must have phrased that wrongly," Courtney said, keeping her voice even. "Thing is I don't remember much of Leah so the both of us will get to know her."

"How does everyone dress for these occasions?" Casey said, her fiery head thrown back against a high backed chair.

"Something with an evening look for dinner. Otherwise casual." Darcy gave her a smile.

"I don't wear dresses a lot," Casey said, just a hint of rebellion in her voice.

"Neither did I," Darcy laughed. "Fact is I've got used to them for certain occasions. Curt loves me in a dress."

"You're a lucky woman, Darcy." Casey looked over at the beautiful creature who was now her sister. "You have a wonderful man who loves you. And I can see you adore him."

"I can't wait to be a married woman," said Darcy and blushed. "Now we're on the subject, Courtney is my maid of honour and two old friends, Fiona Kinsella and Lisa Sanders, are my other bridesmaids but I want you, Casey, to be my bridesmaid too. Will you?" She fixed Casey with a look that said don't-try-to-get-out-of-it.

Casey waited a few moments before she could answer. "I'm too tall," she said. "I'd throw the whole bridal party out of kilter. Just look at Courtney. I tower over her."

"Everyone towers over me." Courtney smiled and touched the top of her shining curls. "Curt and his best man—he's coming at the weekend so you can meet him—are well over six feet. Darcy is tall so is Fee. Lisa is in between. *I'm* the one who should be the drop-out."

"I've never been asked to be a bridesmaid in my entire life," Casey said. "It's an honour, Darcy, but I don't know."

"Look on it as a dress rehearsal for your own wedding," Courtney teased.

Casey tilted her head back and closed her eyes. "I'm never getting married."

"Not even engaged?" Courtney was still teasing.

"I've developed differently to you," Casey said, straightening up. "No man is ever going to get the chance of dumping me."

Adam Maynard stepped briskly out of the lift to catch a bite to eat before his afternoon meeting with the industrialist Sir Arthur Elliot, one of the firm's top clients. His mind was totally preoccupied with a proposal he intended to put before Sir Arthur to save him yet more tax, when a young woman hailed him.

"Adam!"

Out of context at first he didn't know her but he wrenched his mind back. It was that Barbra something who had caused so much angst between him and Courtney at the Polo Ball held on Curt's splendid station, Sunset Downs. She was dressed very differently now and she looked a whole lot better. She wore a very smart outfit in black and white, black strappy sandals, expensive shoulder bag, dark glossy hair longer than he remembered and brushed back to reveal lustrous drop pearl earrings. The kind of young woman any guy would want to date.

"Barbra, isn't it?" he asked with just a touch of derision.

"What a surprise to see you." She gave him an admiring once-over before smiling brightly up into his face. "Especially when we both work at the big end of town. I'm with Cooper-McLaren now," she said.

"Right." He nodded his dark head. He knew the firm. "You'll have to excuse me, Barbra. I'm in one heck of a hurry." He didn't trust this young woman. She was a born troublemaker who had never got over being by-passed for a top job by Courtney McIvor.

Barbra for her part could fairly feel the dislike coming off him. So handsome and well dressed he'd been incredibly easy to spot. Persistence paid off. She loved those dark bedroom eyes intriguingly combined with the cool clipped voice. The contrast was exhilarating. She'd hung around for weeks hoping to run into him. Only a fool would let a guy like Adam Maynard out of her sights. "You still sound cross with me," she said, managing to look deeply hurt. "I wasn't lying, you know, about Courtney. Obviously you all believed her. But she really did brag she was going to wrap her father around her little finger."

Adam met her eyes squarely. "Don't waste my time with lies, Barbra. What is it with you? Can't you contain your jealousy of Courtney? She took your job? Is that it?"

Barbra knew just how to swallow and appear on the verge of tears. "She did take my job, Adam," she said very quietly, looking down momentarily so her dark eyelashes lay on her smooth cheeks. "And threw it away." She looked up earnestly. "Courtney has enormous charm which she uses to maximum effect. I could easily produce a colleague who knew us both well. She'd back my story to the hilt."

Adam tried to get a grip but his patience was fraying. "Barbra, I really am in a big hurry."

"Maybe we could meet up later," she suggested, trying to hold the eagerness down. If she could land a man like this! A handsome guy going places. "I could bring my friend if you need proof. I hate to think someone thinks so badly of me. I may have made a mistake telling tales out of school, Adam, a few drinks loosened my tongue, you know how it is, but believe me *I'm* not the liar. I'm not the one who should be in the line of fire. That's Courtney. She knows exactly how to get people on side. I've studied her, but I can't bring myself to copy her."

"So you've been kind enough to tell us," he answered in a cool voice. "It's just that *I* believe Courtney's version."

"Well why wouldn't you?" Barbra asked sadly. "You're a guy. Courtney attracted guys like bees to the honey pot. She convinced us all blondes have more fun. They beat brunettes hands down."

"That must make you want to see your hair stylist," Adam said. "Look, we can't change what happened. You upset a whole lot of people. My advice to you is the same I used to get from my grandmother. If you can't say something good about someone, say nothing."

"Then people like Courtney McIvor gets away with murder?" Barbra retaliated, jealousy snaking through her body. "The way I heard it she lost no time persuading her dying father to leave her a fortune equal to her big sister's. Nice going!" Barbra looked as though she was about to dissolve into frustrated tears. "If I were you, seeing you're hand-ing out advice, I'd be mighty suspicious of Courtney McIvor's pretty little ways and the baby blues. Underneath it all, she's a cool, calculating bitch."

"How you loved to get your tongue around that," Adam retorted, disdain on his dark handsome face. "I really must go, Barbra. I have a big afternoon coming up."

He sketched a brief salute and continued on his way across the marble lobby and out the door, losing himself swiftly in the lunchtime crowd.

Drat bloody Barbra, he thought, his nerves jangling. The last thing he needed was for all his old doubts about Courtney to resurface. He didn't like lies. He'd given himself over to anticipating this coming weekend at Murraree. He'd missed her. Right then he didn't want to think just how much. Either Barbra was a highly accomplished actress—she really did look like she was about to burst into tears—or Courtney really had leaned heavily on her undeniable charms to get what she wanted. Courtney McIvor might look like an angel but he knew for a fact she had a hard head for business.

Trust came hard to Adam. He had seen too much of deception, sometimes from the most unlikely people. No matter how deeply she moved him Adam made a quick resolution to hold back until he was more sure of her.

* * *

In the end because there was no time to trek off shopping, Darcy came up with an idea for Casey's dinner outfit. A top she'd recently acquired but hadn't yet worn. It was a sleeveless satin wrap top, silvery-blue in colour printed with deep blue peonies in the oriental style. A very wide silver belt held it, pointing up a narrow waist. Casey had her own designer label stretch blue jeans to wear. Her own high heels. Courtney contributed the shell earrings that fell in two lustrous oval discs.

"I loved them when I saw them, but they overwhelm me," she said. "They'll look great on you."

Casey put them on and turned for an inspection. "Well?"

"Just like I said. Terrific."

"So what's on your mind?" Casey took the earrings off and laid them carefully on the table. "You seem a little flustered. You're thinking about the lawyer guy aren't you?"

"No." Courtney's flower face pinked.

"You *are!*" Casey contradicted. "What time does he arrive?"

"Two o'clock if the charter flight is right on time. He landed some big deal so he was able to take today off."

"He must be very smart," Casey said. "He looks it. A full partner in a top firm and he's what, thirty, thirty-one?"

"I think so. I haven't asked him his birthday," Courtney said.

"But you like him?" Casey grinned wickedly. "You don't have to answer."

"I will. It's a lot warmer than liking, but he's not an easy man to know. We got off on the wrong foot. He suspected me of trying to influence the outcome of Dad's will. I tried to explain that was the last thought in my head but I guess it's his job to be suspicious."

"If he can't trust you, don't trust him," Casey advised, picking up her Akubra and cramming it on her head. "I'm joining Darcy at the Four Mile." She glanced at her watch. "Better get going. Reckon I could trust myself on a horse without breaking an arm or a leg?"

"You're already a better rider than I am," Courtney said. Casey had proved a natural like Darcy who had shown her the ropes.

"Threwd her in the dam and she swam, threwd her on a horse and she rode," Casey joked. "See you this afternoon. You're picking up Adam?" Casey's beautiful smile widened.

"Yes and you can take that grin off your face. You're every bit as keen to see Troy Connellan."

"Maybe, but I'm not going to tell *him* that," Casey said.

* * *

The charter flight came in right on time. No waiting around.

"Hi Adam!" *Don't fall to pieces, you idiot!* "How was the trip?"

"Hit a couple of thermals on the last leg," he said, his mouth briefly touching her cheek when he really wanted to sweep her into his arms. "How are you?" Only his eyes drank her in. She was so well proportioned she looked like a perfect figurine. Cool as a vanilla and peach ice cream in the dry desert heat. The little V-neck T-shirt she wore with her white cotton jeans clung to her, barely hiding the contours of her small exquisite breasts. His stomach hardened into a tight knot. She had made astonishing inroads into his life.

Courtney for her part thought those fathomless dark eyes were probably seeking out her sins. She in turn studied him, hoping she wasn't taking overlong. He looked like he'd just stepped out of an advert promoting classy outdoor gear. Sand coloured cotton jacket over a sky-blue and chocolate check shirt, navy cotton jeans, stitched leather tan loafers. He had just the right elegant athletic body to carry it all off.

"I'm fine," she responded automatically, pulling her eyes away and setting off for the Jeep. "Looking forward to the weekend. It's a way of confirming Casey's position in our life and introducing her to our friends. Later, if she's agreeable, we'll do more."

"How's she settling in?" Adam asked, depositing his single suitcase in the back of the vehicle.

"We've bonded remarkably well. She already rides better than I do. I'm not bad, but I'll never be in Darcy's league which Casey might very well be in time. I'm hoping we can persuade her to sing and play for us over the weekend. She's amazing. I can't understand why she hasn't cut a CD."

"I expect she'll get around to it," Adam said. "She's had other things on her mind. Have you and Darcy come to any decision regarding a settlement?"

"A settlement." Courtney swung her shining blond head. "Darcy and I were thinking more of a three-way split."

"We'll have to talk about that," Adam answered noncommittally. "You and Darcy are the only off spring of Jock McIvor's marriage. He named you in his will. At this stage, you and Darcy are the ones in possession. Casey is his natural daughter. Of course she is entitled, both morally and legally, but you don't want to create problems with the title to the station."

"Protecting our interests, Adam?" Courtney asked sweetly, putting the Jeep into gear.

"That's what I'm paid for," he said mildly. "Obviously we have to discuss it. Curt is the executor of your father's estate. I'm only one of the trustees."

"But you're the legal man."

"Yes. Why is it I get the strong impression you don't have a lot of time for legal men?"

She didn't look at him. He made her heart turn over. "Maybe it's because they ask such a lot of money for very little work."

"I hope you're not referring to me, Ms McIvor?" He gave her a hooded look. "I'm waiting."

"No, sir!" There was a ghost of a smile on her lips.

Minutes later they entered the empty house, cool and inviting after the dancing white-heat of the day.

"You have your usual room," Courtney said, leading the way up the staircase to the first floor gallery. She hoped she appeared a whole lot cooler than she felt. Having Adam around made all her nerves feel wired. At his bedroom she turned with a charming little gesture of her hand. "I hope you'll—"

It happened involuntarily. He wasn't even thinking. He was *feeling*. All his careful planning went up like a puff of smoke. He pulled her to him, his mouth shutting off her breath. His arm held her close to his chest. He kissed her hard and fast and deep, surrendering to that overpowering urge.

How long did it last? Courtney felt like she was swooning away. "I'll never understand you," she gasped when she was able, too weak to even push him away.

"How could you? I don't understand myself." He

started kissing her again, burying his face in the sweet scented curve of her neck. He'd told himself he wouldn't *do* this but that was easy to say when he was hundreds of miles away. Bring it down to mere inches and he couldn't help himself. She was too bewitching. He was desperate to trust her all the way but he knew she had real powers of persuasion. At best he'd get burned. At worst, she'd have him eating out of her pretty little hand.

Just like McIvor.

"What are you thinking?" The words came out in a frustrated rush. Her heart was beating double-time. She didn't even feel like she belonged to herself.

He went perfectly still for a moment. "I'm thinking how alluring you are."

She gave a little wince. "Alluring is a problematic word."

"You'd prefer something else?" He lifted his dark head, his lean features taut.

"Something that smacks less of deliberate enticement." Her voice was suddenly angry.

"You *haven't* tried to entice me?" He stared into her sky-coloured eyes.

"Perish the thought!"

"That's okay then." He smiled crookedly. "I don't mind telling you you're succeeding whether you mean to or not." To prove it, he pulled her in tight again, his body separate from his mind.

"You're not going to kiss me again?" She felt nothing but self-disgust at sounding so breathless.

"You know damned well what I need."

"Just remember I didn't ask for it."

"Courtney," he murmured, and touched the skin of her cheek slowly, savouring its texture. Then his mouth came down on hers again, headlong, hungry, questing. Courtney gave up trying for self-control. She thought she would have crumpled only he was holding her up. She wasn't just yielding to *his* need, either. She was yielding to her own.

After a while it was getting so torrid she thought she'd better do something.

She put her hand to his chest. "Wait."

"I've already waited too long." H swept her off her feet, carrying her back to a deep armchair, draping her across his knees.

What *were* those ragged little sounds? Was *she* making them? She couldn't seem to get close enough to him though he was hugging her body tight. Her head supported by his arm was bent over the arm of the chair, the fingers of his other hand playing with her curls. They were acting like a pair of star-crossed lovers parted for a thousand years.

"God," he said, finally lifting his mouth off hers. "How did this happen?" He shook his head sharply as if to clear it.

Courtney let out an explosive little breath. "I'll

tell you how it happened. You grabbed me. And you'd better let me up." She wriggled a little on his lap. Stopped abruptly when she realized what she was doing to him.

"I want to crush you," he said. "I could. You're so small and delicate." He gazed down at her, the limpid eyes, the glowing skin, the sensuous pinkness of her lovely mouth.

"I'm almost tempted to get fat!" Breathing hard she levered herself away from him by pushing hard on his chest. She stood, swaying a little from the force of her emotions. "Your arrogance is staggering! No, don't interrupt. You get worse every time I see you. You can't trust me with anything, either." Her blue eyes flashed. "That's why relationships fail. Do you know that? Lack of trust. No, don't get up," she warned him. "I don't want you looming over me. You already have too much of an advantage."

"You could have fooled me," he said, scraping back a lock of raven hair that had fallen onto his forehead. "Can I help it if I want you?"

"Well we all know with what *part*," she said snappily and took a few small steps away. "I started out showing you your room. Next thing you're into wildly kissing me."

"I could have sworn you enjoyed it," he returned silkily, "to the point of hyperventilating. I'm sorry, Courtney. You look much too sweet to sound as fu-

rious as you do. The sight and scent of you comes
at me with such speed I'm bowled over. It's my only
excuse."

"So it's not your body but your mind that has
made the decision to reject me?"

"My mind doesn't seem to count." He rose to his
commanding height, looking down at her.

She was silent for a while trying to calm herself.
"You're not making complete sense, Adam."

"No, I'm not, am I?" His smile was very white
against his tanned olive skin.

Courtney deliberately took a few more paces
back, as though he might take it into his head to
grab her again. "Obviously you've got problems,"
she said.

"Cheerful thought!" He shrugged. "But I manage
to get by."

"Maybe, but you'll have to make some changes
sooner or later. You can't bear to lose control over
a woman. I've learned that."

"There's not much choice with you," he told her
sardonically. "You're enormously appealing to me.
I can't hide it. But contrary to what you seem to
think, I really want something more than the physical from you."

Courtney felt a surge of pride. "Oh, the physical's
not good enough for you? You want my soul? Have
you also made a vow to reform me? I mean, you've

already labelled me a *fraud.* I manipulated my father. I'm manipulating you. I'm the wicked little temptress. Didn't that bitch of a Barbra tell you as much? She really got to you, didn't she? Maybe you've met up with her around town. That would be easy enough. Compared notes. Have you?" She took a harsh breath at some fleeting shadow across his face. "Casey told me something that makes complete sense. If someone doesn't trust you, don't trust them."

"Maybe we don't know one another well enough for complete trust," Adam offered gently. "Forgive me, Courtney. I didn't aim to upset you. I've only arrived and I feel I should be leaving."

"Not on *my* account!" She swung back, a real chill in her normally gentle voice. "This weekend is meant to be for Casey. I'm not going to be the one to spoil it."

CHAPTER FIVE

BY NOON Saturday morning everyone had arrived, light aircrafts dotting the landing strip like a flock of white birds.

Courtney felt her ragged emotions were perfectly understandable but she kept them well hidden. She wasn't out to spoil anyone's fun. It was great to meet up with Troy Connellan again. He was so *big* and ruggedly handsome she couldn't believe this was the boy she remembered.

He laughed down at her, taking her small hand very gently into his own. "So, Courtney, all grown up. You're beautiful!"

"So are *you!*"

"Haven't grown all that far," Troy's sister, Leah commented. She strolled up, her current boyfriend Paddy Nicholls in tow who Courtney later learned was quite the man around town in Sydney. "You and your half sister will have to get used to cracks about the long and the short of it. How are you, Courtney?" Arctic-blue eyes looked Courtney up and down and apparently found her wanting. "Meet my friend, Paddy. Paddy Nicholls from Sydney. He's staying with us a while."

"Delighted!" Paddy who bore more than a passing resemblance to a dapper English film star, gave the really delicious-looking little blonde a big smile. "I have to thank you for asking me, Courtney. This life you've got out here is quite extraordinary." His light charming speaking voice vibrated with interest and pleasure.

So *he* wasn't going to be a problem, Courtney thought, gracefully disengaging herself, but sister Leah was. Good-looking as she was, although she didn't resemble her golden-bronze big bear of a brother at all, her manner Courtney found quite abrasive. Did Leah really have to start out with barbed comments? She'd do well not to antagonize Casey. She'd lose. Courtney allowed herself a smile at the thought. Casey was fiery and intimidated by no one. It struck her, too, looking around the assembled group, people in the Outback, men and women were much taller and leaner, than they were in the cities.

With relief she turned from Leah to the other young women, grouped around Darcy and Casey who presented a stunning contrast in beautiful women. Darcy's sable head, with her remarkable aquamarine eyes; Casey, a study in alabaster, red and gold with their father's brilliant sapphire eyes. It seemed like a miracle to Courtney, exposed to the Outback sun as she was Casey still hadn't acquired a single freckle though she did take good care of her skin.

Fee Kinsella and Lisa Sanders, both Darcy's age were really nice. No sharp tongues. No assessing eyes. Just warmth and kindness and a desire to be friends. She'd renewed her acquaintance with them briefly at her father's funeral, then more leisurely when they had visited Murraree over the festive season. Both were to be Darcy's bridesmaids. As thrilled about it as was she, Casey as yet hadn't committed. Courtney guessed Casey was waiting to see what this weekend would bring and whether she considered she would fit in.

With the exception of Paddy Nicholls who would probably fit in effortlessly in any gathering, the men knew each other well. Curt and Adam had become good friends, sharing a mutual respect. Troy, Garrett and Stuart Dundas were Curt and Darcy's friends from childhood. Stuart, with his sun bright hair and smiling blue eyes was to be Curt's best man.

The easiest way around lunch was a barbeque where everyone could help themselves. Courtney had saved herself for dinner. Thanks to her mother, all those cooking lessons and her interest in and accumulation of cookery books and videos, she had turned into a very good cook. She actually loved it, the whole thing. The deciding on the menu, the preparation, the presentation. She didn't even mind the washing up, although tidying up as she went along had become an ingrained habit.

More than anything else Courtney wanted her sisters to enjoy this weekend. Her reunion with Darcy after their long years of separation had richly illumined her life. Now Casey had joined them and they didn't want to let her go. Casey had to be compensated for all the years she'd been a frightened and abused child. Not that anyone would ever guess. Courtney looked over to where a wonderfully confident and self-assured appearing Casey was standing laughing happily at something Troy Connellan had said.

Casey was fabulous. Courtney only hoped she could persuade her to sing for them. She was so looking forward to showing her off. Some of Casey's songs she'd written herself had brought tears to her sisters' eyes. They spoke of old grieves both she and Darcy could share.

"Well you've really done up the house," Leah remarked, looking around critically as Courtney ushered her into the allotted guest room. "What decorator did you use?"

Courtney named him. "We all got on remarkably

well. Hugh listened to everything we had to say. We were actually of one mind on just about everything."

"What experience would *you* have?" Leah asked in her faintly jeering way.

"Darcy and I have natural good taste." Courtney met that remark with just the hint of an acerbic note. After all Leah was their guest. "I hope you're comfortable here, Leah. Come down when you're ready. I have to get the barbeque underway."

"You? You look about fifteen," Leah laughed. "Don't run away. I don't bite. I want to ask you something about Casey."

"Ask away!" Courtney's blue eyes began to sparkle.

"I want to hear all about her. Everything."

"Why is that?"

"Because I think she's somehow got her hooks into my brother." Leah sat down on the bed with a worried frown. "He's been acting kind of weird."

"I thought you hardly saw him," Courtney retorted.

Leah gave her a frowning stare. "No need to get on your high horse. Dad and I have plans for Troy. He's as good as promised to Sandra Gordon. Her dad is my dad's best friend. I like Sandra, too."

"I bet she's grateful for that," Courtney said lightly, already making for the door. "If you want to know all about my sister, why don't you ask her yourself?"

"Because she looks totally unpredictable, that's why. Troy has been calling her a goddess. Stuff like that."

"Well, I think myself that just about describes her."

Leah drilled her with another stare. "So you've bonded? Isn't that sweet! And it was all so totally unexpected. I just thought we two could have a quiet chat. I love my brother. I want the best for him."

"Then he couldn't go past someone like Casey," Courtney said, twiddling a little farewell with her fingers. "See you at lunch."

Lunch was a thoroughly relaxing informal affair, easy and carefree, with everyone, with the notable exception of Leah who sat back like a princess expecting to be waited on, pitching in. With the various salads and accompaniments prepared, Courtney found she had little to do but enjoy herself. She looked over to where Adam was busy brushing lamb cutlets with plum sauce as they continued cooking. Lisa was standing beside him, chatting away, clearly revelling in his company. Why not? Adam was an extremely attractive man. And he was unattached. She couldn't blame Lisa for giving it her best shot. She loved the way happiness radiated from Darcy and Curt. That was definitely the *upside* of love. She was experiencing the *downside* herself.

It was then she did a double-take. She couldn't

love Adam Maynard, could she? She was all-out in-fatuated with him. But *love?* Gosh, she would have to think seriously about that.

Paddy Nicholls wedged himself beside her on a stone bench, staring smilingly into her eyes. "I've hardly had a chance to talk to you and I *need* to!"

After lunch settled everyone took to the pool, again with the exception of Leah who lay back in a recliner all afternoon showing off her eye-stopping cut-out one piece black swimsuit that never did get wet.

"I hope you're going to sing for us?" Troy asked Casey, gathering her one armed in the shallow end where Curt had adjusted a huge patio umbrella to give shade, especially to the red-headed Casey who did indeed look like a goddess in a halter necked blue bikini printed with hot pink hibiscus.

"I promised the girls I would," Casey said, toss-ing her long blazing hair over her shoulder. "Your sis-ter's a really nice person. She's twice tried to rile me and succeeded. Next time I'll bop her in the nose."

Troy looked around to where his sister was lying. "I guarantee her nose will never be the same again. Ignore her," he advised. "She thinks I'm a little bit too interested in you."

"I guess you must be," Casey smiled lazily. "Since you've taken to making love to me with your eyes. I've never seen anyone with gold gleaming eyes before."

"You never met my mother," he said. "She had gold eyes."

Casey reached out and gently touched a finger to his mouth. "No, don't. I've made you unhappy. I didn't mean to. I didn't know."

"It's all right." He shook back beads of water from his sunstreaked bronze hair that matched the pelt on his broad dark tanned chest. "I just haven't found the right moment to tell you about my mother, Casey."

"As I recall, we had to be lying in bed together?"

"So how much longer do I have to wait?" he asked huskily, his gaze dropping from her stunning face to the swell of her breasts.

"My guess is a very long time," she taunted. Even now she couldn't escape the past. Her mother had trusted a man. Been seduced and abandoned. Troy Connellan was definitely a man. And what a man! So wonderfully unnervingly masculine. Just as well she knew how to protect herself. Her body if nothing else.

"I'm told women are always changing their minds." He continued to survey her with those mesmerizing eyes.

She splashed him as if to cool him down, then heaved herself effortlessly out of the pool, dangling her long thoroughbred legs in front of him. "Hope then, Connellan. It's not a crime."

While the men played pool, upstairs the young women wandered from bedroom to bedroom catching up on everyone's life. There was a lot of laughter, a lot of banter, at which her sisters were delighted to find Casey joined in. Casey had taken to Darcy's friends, Fee and Lisa on sight, recognising from long practice there wasn't a skerrick of meanness or malice in them. A trait that appeared to distinguish Troy's only sibling. While everyone joined in the fun Leah sat back as was her wont, her expression suggesting she'd gotten over these girly afternoons a very long time ago.

Why had she come? Casey pondered. Obviously not to join in the fun. She's come to check me out and she isn't being all that discreet about it. Where Troy's eyes were pure gold, and his hair ranged from blond to bronze and every tone in between, his sister's eyes were an icy shade of blue, her hair black satin cut in a swinging pageboy. She was certainly arresting but there was nothing remotely friendly about her.

"It's a pity you didn't invite Sandra?" she called to Darcy at one point.

"Sandra Gordon?" Darcy asked. "Maybe next time." It was a diplomatic response. Darcy had never been all that friendly with Sandra.

"Of course you know she's still carrying a torch for Troy. Dad and I are hoping they'll make a match of it."

"I'm sorry, Leah," Darcy said, aquamarine eyes wide. "I didn't know Troy was keen on Sandra?"

"Can I tell you all a secret?" Leah waited for them all to fall silent. "It was fixed long ago. Sandra is special!" At that precise point she fixed her eyes on Casey.

Casey didn't even blink.

Casey stood and surveyed herself in the long mirror, then with a deep breath she turned to go downstairs. She'd already seen Courtney who'd called in on her a few minutes before. Courtney looked perfect. Like the angel on the Christmas tree. She wore white, top and full skirt, banded and embroidered in gold. Darcy had swept in, just as she was applying her makeup. Darcy's outfit again was two piece. A green-aqua printed silk georgette skirt that flowed around her long legs, the camisole a beautiful aqua that matched her eyes. Darcy moved with such a spring in her step Casey found it a pleasure just to watch her. Darcy had had her bad times but her future looked rosy. Casey checked the lump in her throat. She hadn't expected her half sisters to embrace her—pretty much figuring they'd resent her—instead they had welcomed her with open arms and closed ranks behind her.

So everything has turned out just fine!

It was cause for wonderment. Just when she thought there were no miracles in life one had happened. And there was one in the offing, Troy Connellan. She knew she wanted love desperately. She wanted warmth and approval and companionship. She was getting that from her sisters. But to embark on life's great adventure? To become a wife and mother. For that she needed a man. A *real* man.

Smiling faces down the length of the gleaming dinner table. Darcy at one end. Curt at the other. Casey on Darcy's right. Adam opposite her. Courtney on Curt's right, Troy opposite her. The others within touching distance. The table setting was a work of art Casey thought, studying everything that went on around her. Beautiful bone china, sparkling crystal, gleaming silverware. She wasn't used to this at all. Then again it wouldn't be all that hard to get used to. She had an inherent love of beautiful things. The overhead chandelier was on the dimmer, soft, flattering light coming from the glow of candles in silver candlesticks positioned down the table.

Courtney had created a truly beautiful centre piece made up of yellow waterlily buds, a graceful curve of narrow leaves, minute cream terrestrial orchids and some small royal purple flowers that looked like iris but were in fact native to Murraree's lagoons. Courtney was very accomplished Casey thought. She produced beautiful meals effortlessly. She ran what was a very large house and kept it looking wonderful. Lately she had set about training two young aboriginal girls to work around the house and help in the kitchen. She did all the ordering of supplies, she balanced the books. She was listening to something the guy from Sydney—Paddy Nicholls—was saying, her expression absorbed, her blonde head tilted towards him as if he were the most interesting man in the world. She was so small and delicate albeit full of energy, beside her Casey felt like one of those blue cranes, the brolgas, that performed their fantastic ballets around the billabong flats.

Other eyes but hers were observing Courtney as though drawn by powerful magnets. Adam Maynard, for one, though he covered it well. He continued to smile and contribute to the conversation in his smooth sophisticated fashion. But the real focus of his attention was Courtney. What was going on behind those dark eyes? Casey wondered. There was intimacy between Courtney and Adam but it was complicated. Starting a relationship was like a trip into the great unknown.

Further down the table Troy's sister, the unlovable Leah was drinking her wine very quickly. She set down the crystal glass so hard Casey almost expected the long stem to break. She stared across the table with a tense jaw, obviously supremely irritated at the way her boyfriend was responding to Courtney's silken attractions. Casey knew the signs. Paddy Nicholls was finding Courtney extraordinarily attractive. Not only was she lovely in every respect; she was one of the McIvor heiresses who had received quite a lot of press. Perhaps the charming witty Paddy couldn't envisage life without a rich wife. Why else would he be with Leah?

At least that's taken the heat off me, Casey thought, baffled by why Connellan Senior would favour Leah over Troy when Leah, for all her obvious attractions, was a real pain in the ass. The spoiled rotten daughter of a rich man who had never had a job.

"Why would I want to *work?*" she had hooted, when Lisa had asked her what on earth did she do with herself? "I've got a rich dad who loves me!"

Apparently "Dad" didn't indulge his only son. Both Curt and Darcy had told her Troy worked extremely hard, but they hadn't divulged his story. By the sounds of it, it was right out of a black closet. Casey realized she wanted to hear it so much she was actually considering Troy's proposition. She'd even begun fantasizing about her and Troy tucked up together in a big comfortable bed.

She caught her breath. Exhaled. It was nice of

Leah to warn her Troy had the perfect wife-to-be tucked away. What was her name? Sandra something. Ah, yes, Sandra Gordon.

"It's high time Troy settled down!" Leah, eighteen months his junior had pointed out. "Start a family. Dad needs grandkids."

"You can provide him with that!" Darcy had reminded her.

The answer: "Hell, no! I'm having too much fun."

What if I held out my heart to him? Casey thought. What if he refused it? What if he used and abused it? There's no safety in love affairs. Desire blurred all thought of caution. One false move and life could never be the same again.

Afterwards there was dancing in the cool of the terrace. The pool was floodlit, the water the translucent aqua of Darcy's eyes. Courtney saw Darcy and Curt move into one another's arms. Lovers coming home. Darcy rested her temple against his chin. Their love for each other was so radiant it created some kind of force field around them. Courtney wondered if she and Casey would ever be blessed with a love like that. She knew deep inside her she had already met a man she wanted to love her. She wasn't such a fool she didn't know he was more than half way *in* love with her. Getting him to *love* her was far harder. He had confessed how one woman had betrayed his trust. It was quite possible he still hadn't worked *that* one out. Trust, she knew, was very important to Adam.

"Hey!" His clean breath touched her cheek as he bent his dark head to her. "What's going on? Not dancing or are you waiting for Paddy? He's rather smitten."

"I've been trying hard to attract him."

She shimmered before him. Her hair shimmered, her eyes, her skin, her dress. The upward tilt of her delicately determined chin let Adam know her hostility hadn't diminished.

"Well you're certainly distracting him," Adam pointed out, his tone deepening with humour. "Could I perhaps bully you into a dance?" he mocked, then without waiting for an answer, he lightly encircled her waist, drawing her away from the vine wreathed pillar that had framed her.

She let him, her expression cool as a lily, underneath coping with a surge of excitement. Wasn't she *yearning* to be in his arms, hypocrite that she was! Try coping with that!

"That's a lovely dress. I've never seen it before." He gazed down at her, thinking she looked exquisite. He also knew she was determined not to give him whatever he wanted. Her pride required it.

"I kept it just for you," she smiled up at him sweetly, sarcasm in her eyes.

"Now, now," he chided. "I've forgotten about our little spat. Why don't you?"

"Because I know it's going to start up again sometime soon. Just as a matter of interest, *have* you run into my dear friend, Barbra in Brisbane? More likely she hunted you."

"You don't expect a yes to that?" he asked laconically.

"Aren't you a man who demands the truth? Whereas I lie effortlessly."

"Don't, Courtney." He turned her with one fluid movement to avoid bumping into Leah and Paddy who appeared to be having their own confrontation. "You're a beautiful, graceful dancer. Anyone would think we'd be practising together."

His own rhythms and instincts were excellent, Courtney thought but she wasn't to be put off. She was aware Adam had been watching her closely at dinner even if no one else saw it. Maybe Casey. Casey's sapphire eyes had been busy sizing them all up. "Had you arranged to meet? Did Barbra promise you she'd bring along her friend, Gillian, to back her story? Gillian's another one who hated being passed over. Just a yes or a no. That's all I ask."

"Then will you stop?" Adam stared into her sparkling eyes, trying hard to maintain a calm exterior. "It's such a beautiful night. I have a beautiful girl in my arms. Dinner was marvellous by the way. You're a very accomplished young woman."

"Forget the distractions. Well?" she probed.

"Yes or no! One's the right answer. The other isn't."

"So it's a yes?" Courtney guessed correctly, not needing his confirmation, which in fact he didn't supply.

Adam groaned. "Barbra waylaid me in the lobby of our office building. Personally I think she's more interested in *me* than you. I don't like to sound big-headed, but a lot of women find me attractive."

"It's like water off a duck's back to you, isn't it? Master of your own fate. Your standards are exceptionally high. Of course she created a very bad impression at the Polo Ball so she had to re-establish herself with you as a solid citizen. In the process she dished up more dirt on Courtney McIvor, the man-eater?"

Adam looked down at her with his brooding dark eyes. "I make a living out of dealing with all sorts of people in a civilised way, Courtney. Actually I was a little cool with Barbra. I told her I had a big afternoon coming up, which I did and went on my way. Satisfied?"

She bit her lip. "You've told me enough. Trust counts for a lot. Your ex-girlfriend—the one who lived in—the one who cheated on you did a lot of damage."

"A man has his pride, Courtney," he said dryly. "What you have to do now is relax." He pulled her in closer, wanting to pick her up and spirit her away. It would be easy enough. "Let's go for a ride in the morning. Up to it? I mean early. Say around six?"

"I have to get breakfast," she lamented, thereby betraying her desire to join him.

"You don't *have* to do anything. With the possible exception of Leah, your girlfriends seem pretty capable to me."

"Of course they are. It's just that—"

"Forget it," he said. "In any case we'll be back."

"Ride as in horses?" The mistress of any number of intricate dance steps, Courtney actually stumbled, provoking a mocking "ouch!"

"That was the idea unless you'd prefer to take one of the vehicles."

"No, a horse is fine just so long as it's not Tango," Courtney said wryly, recalling how she had taken a tumble from the part-thoroughbred filly. "No good putting me on a hot-tempered horse. I'm not a good enough rider, though Darcy keeps telling me how much I've come on. I'm afraid my father did such a good job of undermining my confidence I'll need time to get over it. Casey now is a natural. I think she could stay put on anything."

Adam could well see it. Casey looked one spunky, take-no-nonsense young woman. Horses had the natural ability to take the measure of the rider. If the rider was nervous the horse knew straight away. Similarly, confidence was a big part of getting the best out of a horse. An excellent rider himself, sympathetic to Courtney's problem caused by the insensitivity of her late father, Adam thought he could offer her some good advice. His main aim, however, was not so altruistic. He was desperate for them to be on their own.

When Darcy asked Casey would she sing for them, Casey responded at once. Apart from ignoring Leah's somewhat blatant attempts to scuttle any relationship she might be thinking of embarking upon with her brother, the evening had been a great success. Dancing with Troy the enjoyment had increased one hundred fold. Despite his size—Troy was a *big* man—he was as light on his feet as a cat. A *big* cat. Usually Casey looked down on a lot of guys. It was remarkably satisfying looking up.

Because everyone was in such a mellow mood she began with a couple of crowd pleasers that caught them up and had them clapping their hands.

Troy had never doubted for a moment they would love her. Casey had star quality. And that was the danger. Her talent could take her away from him. She only had to cut a CD, have *one* hit and she'd move on. He realised he wasn't going to get out of this unscathed. McGuire had got to him. Casey McGuire-McIvor. Leah was no fool. She knew as only women did, Sandra Gordon, the family choice, was out of the running.

"Sing 'Song for Marnie'," he called to her. The last time she had sung it he'd been incredibly moved. Powerful emotions had flowed from her to him. He wanted to tell her about his own beautiful mother. About the cloud that hung over her memory.

She leaned towards him, the expression on her face that of the true artist. "If I can."

"You can." He felt he could support her through anything. With everything he had.

"What do you mean?" Leah asked, sharp as a knife. She looked from one to the other. Wasn't it enough this Casey was knock-em-dead stunning, Jock McIvor's illegitimate daughter, she was a wonderful singer who made the guitar talk. Worse, Leah felt her brother Troy, was wild about her.

"It's a sad song, that's all," Casey said

"Sad song! Sad songs are fantastic!" Paddy Nicholls exclaimed, absolutely delighted with this marvellous new turn of events. These McIvor women were really something. Talk about the Three Graces! Brunette, redhead, blonde. All beautiful enough to make a man grovel. Besides, always on the look-out for a business opportunity, Paddy thought there could be something in it for him. "I know people in Sydney who'd love to have you on their books, Casey," he told her. "Glenn Gardiner is a pal of mine." He named a top flight theatrical entrepreneur. "I could introduce you."

"He could, too!" Leah actually smiled. "Glenn would sign you up in a minute." Now suddenly there was a way to get rid of this Casey. Their father would be mighty upset if Troy didn't toe the line and marry Sandra. But then Troy had been refusing point blank to toe the line since they had lost their mother. From then on he'd been in open rebellion against their father giving her the opportunity to win their father's affection.

"You're as good as I've heard, Casey," she added enthusiastically, hoping her big smile was on straight.

"Better," said her brother, giving Casey a long gleaming you-and-me look.

"'Song for Marnie' if you would, Casey," Darcy requested gently, not at that moment knowing if Marnie was a real person or not. How could she? Casey had always found talking about her mother too deeply disturbing. She had never mentioned her mother's Christian name to Darcy or Courtney.

Casey sat on the high stool Troy quickly found her.

Hell, he was behaving like her manager, Leah thought, torn between jealousy and fascination.

There she was, the new woman in Troy's life. A stunning-looking redhead in tight designer jeans with the contrast of a gleaming very womanly satin wrap top that showed off the contours of her beautiful breasts. High heeled black slingbacks were on her feet. No trying to lessen her height, she seemed to flaunt it. Her magnificent red-gold-copper-apricot coloured hair—the lot—fell over one shoulder and tumbled down her back in lush deep waves. Her shallow cleft chin pointed up the beauty and strength of her bone structure. Her startling sapphire eyes were veiled by her sweeping eyelashes as she bent over the guitar, her long fingers plucking strings as she strummed random chords.

Finally she looked up. Her gaze homed in on Troy's. "This is for my mother," she said. It was not by design those words came out. It was more the effect of having Troy's mesmerising golden eyes rest in hers.

The bright songs had beguiled them. The sad song they reacted to in different ways. All were enormously affected. Those that still had their mother which was everyone with the exception of Troy, Leah and Adam, felt blessed by that fact. The throbbing emotion in Casey's low rich voice conveyed to them in losing her mother Casey's heart had been ripped apart.

When she finished Casey raked her tumbling hair back from her face. Her sapphire eyes were extraordinarily brilliant.

For long moments her small audience sat spellbound, then they began to applaud not with the ex-hilaration of her previous two songs but with quiet deep appreciation.

Courtney unashamedly let the tears stand in her eyes. "That was beautiful, Casey," she breathed, profoundly moved by singer and song. "Song for Marnie" was rather like "Danny Boy". She couldn't listen to "Danny Boy" without crying. Both songs broke her heart.

"I'd do *anything* to be able to sing like you," Lisa who had tried her hand at Country and Western moaned. "Paddy's right. You have a big career com-ing up."

Sitting on the couch beside Courtney, Adam felt the light trembling throughout her delicate body. He wanted to pull her across his knees. Cradle her to him. Kiss her tender, sensitive mouth. How well he understood her tears. He thought her tears as lovely as pearl drops. "Song for Marnie" had upset him to the point he was afraid he wouldn't be able to control the on-rush of all the old pain. Like Casey he knew all about agony. He had experi-enced the tragic death of his mother firsthand as had Casey. They had been *there*.

"You're an artist, Casey." Quietly he saluted her, taking a clean handkerchief from his pocket and passing it to Courtney who straightaway dabbed at her drowning blue eyes.

"If I were you, Casey," Leah called in a tight voice, for she, too, had been gripped by emotion, "I'd take Paddy up on his offer. You'll bypass the hassle of trying to establish yourself. Paddy can organise things as soon as he gets back to Sydney. I'm going with him. I think it's pretty clear to all of us you have a big future."

So where does that leave me, Troy thought, his golden eyes still locked on Casey

Open the cage and the beautiful bird flies away.

CHAPTER SIX

SUNUP presented its own magic. In the east a majestic ball of fire rose above the horizon sending long rays of golden light spearing across the desert. The air as yet was wonderfully crisp, deliciously scented by the feathery acacias and so clear everything had a knife edge delineation like a giant film set newly painted. A small group of tan-red kangaroos watched them ride by, the curious angle of their heads and their wonderfully expressive body language suggesting they were eagerly expecting a team of riders to follow.

The birdsong was unbelievable—impossible to separate the different voices—squadron after squadron winging and shrieking overhead. From the lagoons, the billabongs and water holes that criss-crossed the station water birds rose with a mighty thunder of wings. The Channel Country was a major breeding ground for nomadic water birds. In the reed and lily shadowed swamps the Ibis built their nests. The Ibis were the friends of the cattlemen because their huge flocks arrived just in time to feast on the grasshoppers that would otherwise strip bare valuable herbage for the cattle.

In the remote swamps far from prying human eyes the pelicans built their nests. Pelicans were great flyers. They could be seen across the landscape soaring to great heights then hovering on rising thermals so they could spot the best waterholes. But the great sights of the Outback were the millions of chattering budgerigars, the white corellas and the galahs in their pink and grey suits.

Adam pointed to the sky already deepening to a smouldering blue. "I've never seen so many ducks in my life. There must be thousands of them."

"Tens of thousands more like," Courtney corrected, shading her eyes to look up. "One of my earliest memories is the arrival of the Whistling Tree Ducks. They cover the swamps like wall to wall carpets. If you were feather-light you could walk across the lagoons on their backs. On moonlight nights they have a tendency to mistake shining roof tops for moonlit waters and land with a mighty *thunk!*"

"I've heard that," he said. "Casey could write a lot of songs out here. Quiet waters might calm her soul. Speaking of waters, why don't we take a breather over there." He pointed off to the left. Through a screen of bauhinias the sun bounced off a broad sheet of water turning the surface to pure silver.

Don't start getting nervous. Nervous women make mistakes. "Lovely!" she said, following his lead. The bauhinias, the butterfly trees, in springtime flower, white, pink or cerise, were one of her favourite sights.

They dismounted, leaving their horses in the shade to bend their glossy necks to munch pale green sweet succulents. A shore of yellowish sand surrounded the quiet lagoon where cream water-lilies held their exquisite heads high above their dark green pads and the sparkling beauty of the crystal water. Fresh animal tracks leading down to the water were perfectly printed on the bone dry sands.

"I don't know why you say you're not a good rider," Adam remarked, thinking she looked immaculate in her riding gear. "You *can* ride and quite well." They had in fact covered a lot of ground, giving the horses their head in an exhilarating gallop that gave Courtney no trouble.

"Call it choice of mount," she laughed, glancing back at her deep chestnut mare. "Lady Lucy is more than just a pretty face. She has the sweetest disposition. I wouldn't saddle up Starlight." She referred to Adam's spirited choice.

"Starlight's a wonderful horse," Adam said lazily, lowering himself to the sand and holding out his hand to her.

She took it. Briskly let it go. Violent delights have violent ends. "Definitely. He's also temperamental."

"And too big for you by more than a full hand," Adam said. "It's a good idea to match horse to rider." He rested back on one elbow, discarding his Akubra, grateful for the shade. "Sometimes I think I did the wrong thing not taking over my granddad's property. I wanted to set the world on fire. I had a good brain. I wanted to use it. I have no regrets, but all the while I find myself wanting something else. Practising law has given me a sense of achievement and exponentially put quite a lot of money in my pocket but coming out here so often reminds me how much I love the land. How much I miss it. The great peace and freedom it provides. I particularly love the Channel Country. The riverine desert has a rare magic."

"Sounds like you've fallen in love?" she murmured.

"I can't hide it." He turned his lean handsome face towards her, something in his eyes causing her heart to flutter like leaves in a strong breeze.

She took refuge in talk. "Are you saying some time down the track you might abandon legal practice for another career?"

He shrugged. "It happens. At the moment I'm just saying I'm looking for answers. I'm looking for a life of value. Not chasing paper trails and pulling off corporate deals that can be met within

the law. Many of my clients are highly intelligent
people who prize ruthlessness. Ruthlessness gets
them what they want. It's not so much a question
of money but *power* though obviously you need
one to get the other. I like to think I have some of
my spiritual aspirations intact. It was the way I was
raised. Curt is a man I admire. He's quite remarkable. To a certain extent he's buoyed by his family
name, the trust and the goodwill that generates, but
he's both a mover and a visionary. Already a force
within the industry. This country needs men like
Curt Berenger."

"I agree. But do you see yourself as a cattle
baron?" Courtney asked, struck by a fantastic idea
she was sure she'd better keep to herself. "It's not
an easy life though I'm absolutely certain you could
master it."

"Nothing really worthwhile is easy, Courtney.
We both know that. Out here it's survival or go
under. Today's cattleman has to be an excellent
business man. Even Curt turns to me from time to
time for professional help. Come to that I have a
few ideas we should all discuss about running Murraree better. Then there's the matter of Casey. The
wrong that was done to her has to be put right. I expect she'll make her own life. She's very gifted."

A kind of sadness flooded her. "Casey is gifted—
I'm sure Paddy's entrepreneur friend could make

her a big star, but I don't want her to go away. Neither does Darcy. I'm pretty sure Troy Connellan doesn't want her to go away, either, even if his sister can't wait to see the back of her. Casey presents a threat to Leah and her father's plans."

"Troy and Casey?" Adam asked with faint surprise in his voice.

"Hadn't you noticed?" She picked up a handful of sand, ran it through her fingers. "The air hums around them."

"I thought it fairly crackles around us," he said dryly. "Then again I've been too busy watching you to watch them. But now that you mention it there *is* some understanding between the two of them but they've only just met."

"Whoever loved that loved not at first sight?" she asked, giving him a brief slanting look.

"I think there's a warning attached to that," he reminded her. "Too rash, too unadvised, too sudden. Too like the lightning, which doth cease to be."

"You don't think love lasts?" A real desire to know was in her voice.

"I'm sure it does," he affirmed. "True love never dies. The only trouble is not all that many people experience it when love is central to harmonious life. My mother thought she loved me. In the end she chose not to live without my father. They were inseparable from the time they met in their teens.

Then again there was the horrible way my father died rescuing us from the fire. She couldn't handle it. She knows what I would have done without my wise, loving grandparents. My mother had a break-down from which she never really recovered."

Her heart sank. "Adam, I am so, so, sorry." Ready tears sprang into her eyes. She was passionately in love with this complex man.

Adam's dark handsome face was intense, his eyes looking sightlessly straight ahead, full of the grief that years later hadn't really relented. "I found her. She did what severely depressed women often do. She overdosed on her medication."

Courtney had suspected as much, still it came as a shock. "Is it possible she didn't mean to, Adam?" she asked. "Maybe she thought she needed a larger amount to help her through a particularly bad time?"

He forced himself to speak normally. "There was some doubt about it at the time. My grandmother always said it was an accident. She was convinced my mother wouldn't have left me even knowing I'd be well looked after. I suffered, too, losing my fa-ther. He was my hero. A marvellous man. We were great *friends*."

"Did you never consider the accident theory yourself, Adam?" she asked, not only thinking it would lessen his pain, but chances were that was what really happened. "Living with so much grief your mother wouldn't have been exactly *clear* in her mind. She shook out too many tablets and in a cloud of misery swallowed them down. Then she simply went to sleep undisturbed."

His voice was tight. "I have to confess I've mostly believed my mother wanted to be with my father. Not me."

"Does that fit?" She didn't dare touch him. "Did your mother try hard to get home to you after she was hospitalised? I assume she was."

There was a fissure in the grimness of his expression rather like a ray of hope. "She *did*. She was very concerned about me as she always was. My father and I adored my mother. We would have done anything for her."

"Your father did. He saved her life. And yours. Maybe your grandmother was right, Adam. It really was an accident."

He sighed deeply. "We'll never know. Even if I did know for sure, nothing can bring her back."

"But it might work for the good," Courtney insisted. "It would influence your thinking. Soften your memories. After such a terrible tragedy your mother was in a very fragile state of mind. I've done a few funny things I normally wouldn't do when I haven't had my mind on what I was doing. I suppose we all have. If I were you, Adam, I'd trust your grandmother. You did say she was a wise person?"

"She was." His voice softened.

"Do you think she would have *lied* to you even for the best of reasons?" Small wonder Adam had such difficulty with *trust*.

"I don't know," he said wearily, at the same time stirred by hope. "My grandmother was as straight as a die. She shaped me."

"You could trust her," Courtney suggested very gently. "It won't cure your grief but you'll be able to think about your mother in the old way. The loving, protective mother she was before tragedy struck. The efforts she made to regain control. I don't think she would have deliberately chosen to leave her adored son."

There was silence for the space of a full minute. Then he turned to her. "The way you put it, how can I not believe you, or my grandmother? You're wonderfully persuasive, lovely Courtney. The shadings in your gentle voice, the tender expression in your beautiful blue eyes. When I look into them, I can believe anything."

Was that irony? Whatever it was she reacted. "You worry me, Adam. You really do." Those black eyes were intent but she couldn't read them. She made a swift movement to stand up, but he pulled her back onto the sand, one enveloping arm beneath her as she lay.

"No, don't go."

She saw the desire in his eyes.

"I want to kiss you. I want to make love to you. Oh, how I want that! I want to inhale you." He dipped his face to hers, his mouth travelling across the satiny heated skin of her cheeks, his teeth nibbling on the small lobes of her ears. "You're delicious. I could *eat* you."

"Oh, yes, you can eat me!" she fired, putting up her hands, trying to hold him off. "But you can't trust me. That would require a *huge* quantum leap. Though really I understand, Adam. I do. You were terribly injured and you haven't healed."

"So heal me," he growled. "If anyone could, it's *you!*"

His mouth fell upon hers, so passionate an answering desire devoured her. She was fighting him, kissing him, fighting herself, while all the while he continued to rain kisses on her with sweet fierce abandon. His hand shifted to her breast, shaped it, taking its delicate weight. His fingers moved into the V-neck of her shirt, popped a button so he could stroke her creamy flesh.

"You're so beautiful!" His tone was harsh, yet velvety, powerfully seductive. Now his fingertips ran in under the fabric of her bra seeking her rosy erect nipple.

Excitement hit. So violent, so white hot she almost took off like a sky-rocket.

We're all alone. No one will find us.

She wanted him to cover her right there and then. The more time passed, the more he meant to her. The more she needed him. Her body needed him. Oh, how much! She might as well admit she was *lost*.

His mouth found her breast and she abandoned herself to pure sensation. It radiated through her with the heat of golden sunshine. She could smell the flowering earth rise all around them like incense, breathe in the fresh green air. Passion was a fever, a sickness, but it was irresistible.

She wanted to love Adam. She wanted him to love her. He could kiss her forever, pull all her strings, melt her like chocolate, but that didn't prove he *loved* her. Until he'd learned to *trust* her she didn't know if he could.

She was almost weeping with the effort of rolling away from him, out of his reach.

"What's wrong? What's gone wrong?" he asked urgently, watching her sit up, re-hook her pretty flimsy bra and pull the edges of her shirt together.

"Nothing's gone wrong, Adam," she said, breathing fast. "Not *yet!*"

He was breathing hard. Just like her. "You surely didn't think I would *force* you?" There was anger and wounded pride in his dark eyes. "Can't you see I would never hurt you?"

"I need to make sure, Adam," she said, standing up and tucking her shirt into her cream jodhpurs.

"What the hell does that mean? For God's sake, Courtney, is this a game?"

"No games, Adam. Not at all. I want something from you you don't seem able to give."

He stood up, towering over her. "Tell me," he enunciated very carefully.

"I'm trying to understand you, Adam. I'm trying very hard to understand how you think. You told me about the tragedy in your life. I know what it did to you. You had a girlfriend who probably broke your heart when she cheated on you—"

"She didn't," he cut in, his voice hard.

"But you cared about her, didn't you? It must have been a fairly intense relationship for you both to live together?"

"All right, I cared about her. But I never loved her. I'd never have let her go if I'd loved her."

"I don't know about that, Adam," she protested. "I think you'd never forgive any woman for betraying your trust. I know you're *in* love with me. I can't hide the fact it's the same way with me. We *want* each other. But despite everything part of you thinks I could be a sweet talking con woman. A liar in other words. The quintessential blue eyed blonde who manipulates men. Soft as marshmallow on the outside, inside sharp as a tack."

"The fact is you *are* as sharp as a tack," he said ngrily. "You can get the better of me any day."

It was all a question of escape or succumb. "I'm eady to go home," she announced jaggedly, the itter taste of salty tears already in her throat Now!" She threw out an arm as if she were in an ver-powering rush.

"Okay," he replied through his teeth, making a ecisive move back to the horses. "That's the last me you'll dismiss me with a wave of your hand."

How could two people who wanted each other esperately hold themselves so far apart? Lovers nd enemies. The answer lay in the strains and presures of the past.

addy Nicholls lost no time setting up a meeting beween Casey and his high flying pal, the entrepreeur Glenn Gardiner.

"It's a wonderful opportunity, Casey," Darcy said fter they were told the news. "Courtney and I are rilled for you. He'll want to hear you sing. What ongs have you got in mind?"

Casey began to list a few. Some country classics, thers her own material.

"I bet he's going to love you," Courtney said. You have something that sets you right apart. /hat's more your own songs are beautiful. What's

the matter, don't you feel like going?" Strangely
Casey didn't appear to be overjoyed.

Casey shook herself, trying to free herself from
some emotional trap. "Of course I do," she said,
suddenly breaking into a smile. "It's what I've
wanted for years but I've been honing my skills.
guess I'm ready."

"You sure are!" Her sisters confirmed.

"What about your wardrobe?" Courtney studied
Casey's tall lithe body, the long elegant build.

"I guess I should look good."

"That won't be hard," Darcy smiled. "You have
money at your disposal. Credit cards. That's all
been taken care of. I'd get there a couple of days
early if I were you. Do some shopping. First off, we
have to arrange a charter flight to connect up with
your domestic flight…."

It seemed like a roomful of people were waiting
for her. The meeting place was a big name recording studio on the fringe of the city.

Paddy Nicholls stood up, his charming face
wreathed in a boyish smile.

"Casey! Lovely to see you!" He came towards her
holding out arms wide enough for a group hug. If
that weren't enough next she was kissed Euro style.

It was all because she looked terrific! Paddy was
delighted she had lived up to his glowing spiel.
Casey McGuire-McIvor was an agent's dream. An

the outfit was right on without going over the top. Turquoise silk shirt with a satin trim. Turquoise silk-satin jacket with the long sleeves pushed up. Beautifully cut toning pants she wore to perfection. Her make-up was perfect. Her hair a glorious red-gold mane. She'd done him proud!

A good-looking mature man Casey recognised as Glenn Gardiner joined them, his hand stuck out in a greeting.

"Glenn Gardiner, Casey. Good to meet you."

"Good to meet you, Mr Gardiner." She sounded poised, confident when in reality she was nervous.

"Glenn, please," he said affably. When she'd seen him on television she'd thought he sounded like a really nice person. Not cocky or full of himself at all. Nothing flashy. He was well dressed, prosperous-looking, pleasant.

"Let's just say you're even more stunning than Paddy told us." He turned, extending a hand towards the several people in the room. "Let me introduce you to these people. They're in the business. Jake, Ben and Matt are top musicians. They can back you or you can back yourself. Either way we're looking forward to hearing what you can do."

In the end backed by the three top flight musicians she gave a bravura performance. It must have been because it put a big smile on everyone's faces.

And these were people who would only tell you you were good when you were *great!*

"I tell you what, Casey, you're *amazing!*" Matt, the lanky guy with the shoulder length hair and the little goatee told her. "How come I've never heard of you?"

"It takes a little time, Matt."

"Not any more," Paddy was bouncing the soft pads of his fingers together as though he had already negotiated a piece of the action. "With Glenn to manage you, you're on your way."

Glenn stayed another twenty minutes before he had to leave. The contract was discussed. Did she have a lawyer?

Of course she did. Adam Maynard. Courtney was head over heels in love with him but she acted like she didn't want it to get around.

In the end Paddy drove her back to her hotel in the city. Five star. She hadn't stopped spending money. "It'd be nice if we could have dinner?"

What was wrong with her all of a sudden? Couldn't she say yes. Paddy really was charming and he had gone out of his way to help her. It's not as though they intended to jump into bed together afterwards. Well…probably *he* did but she didn't.

"That would have been lovely, Paddy," she lied smoothly, "but I've made plans to catch up with an old friend."

"Another time." Paddy smiled. "In any case we'll be in touch." Six-foot Casey was absolutely stunning but the one who had really captivated him was that adorable little package, Courtney. Being on the good side of Casey would automatically put him on the good side of her sister, half sister, whatever. All of them were heiresses. Paddy had vowed a few years back he'd marry one. His chances were better than most. He mixed with all the right people.

The rest of the day Casey spent wandering around the city. She loved Sydney. No other city in Australia was like it, not simply because of its magnificent sparkling blue harbour; the Bridge that dominated the skyline, the unofficial symbol of the city all over the world; or the Opera House, a great architectural achievement with its white sails glistening in the glorious sunshine. Sydney was a powerhouse, its dynamism reflected in the mood of the people who knew they enjoyed a lifestyle hard to beat.

It was an incredible feeling to have so much money at her disposal, not that it made her gloriously happy. She'd give it all back to have her mother with her. Had she been given a chance she would have been able to look after her mother but fate decreed otherwise.

She was waiting for an elevator to arrive to take her up to her room when a voice hailed her.

"Casey! How did it go?"

Casey turned as Leah Connellan hurried up to her. "Hey, you look great!" she said, her eyes darting all over Casey's classy outfit like a wasp deciding where to land.

"Thank you. You do, too," Casey said, observing the pleasantries.

"Paddy actually wanted me to be there, but I couldn't get out of another appointment."

By the look of it, her hairdresser. Leah's brunette bob was cut and styled to perfection.

"It went very well," Casey said, hoping against hope Leah wasn't staying in the hotel. "I've thanked Paddy for making it possible." *And he asked me to dinner!*

"That's great!" Leah renewed her smile, but somehow it looked false. "You could be the find of the decade. You've got what it takes to make the big time. Who knows you might even get the opportunity to make a name for yourself in the U.S."

Which should be far enough away.

"Are you staying here, Leah?" Casey asked, already resigned.

Leah nodded. "Dad and I. Dad's here to buy me an apartment. I can't think why he hasn't done it before. I need a city pad."

The elevator arrived and they stepped in. "Any date set for signing a contract?" Leah asked, now studying Casey's designer handbag.

"The contract was discussed. I'll have Adam Maynard look over it before I sign it," Casey said.

"You don't exactly sound thrilled?" Leah stared in to the depths of Casey's eyes, fishing for a reason.

"I never sound thrilled, Leah, even when I am. But I was very pleased at the way things went. Ah, my floor coming up. You're going to the penthouse?"

"Yes." Leah gave her a *where-else?* look.

"Nice to see you."

Casey stepped out, waiting for the elevator door to close before rolling her eyes. Leah's friendliness was prompted by relief. The very last thing Leah wanted was for Casey to stick around.

She'd just emerged from the shower when someone knocked on the door. Didn't anyone take any notice of the Do Not Disturb sign? She prayed it wasn't Leah with a surprise invitation to join her and Daddy for dinner. Didn't seem likely. Quickly she shouldered into the hotel's towelling robe, belted it tight around her and opened the door a way ready to head butt anyone who looked at all suspicious.

Instead Troy Connellan stood there, looking absolutely marvellous in his city clothes, a smile on his handsome rugged face. "Hi, there! Stay here often?"

"First time."

He nodded, golden eyes gleaming. "I wasn't even

aware you were in Sydney until ten minutes ago. Can I come in?"

"Say no more." Casually she held back the door with nothing to indicate what his surprise appearance meant to her. Thrills had been rare in Casey's life. Troy Connellan sent so many shock waves up and down her spine she almost dropped to her knees.

"Leah told you?" She trailed him in, in the wake of his blazing vitality. He couldn't be anything else but an outdoors man. He brought the fresh clean tang of the outdoors in.

He reached for a chair, sat in it, looked out the window at the view of the park. "Definitely not Leah. She failed to mention it." There was a dry edge to his voice. "I happened to run into that friend of hers, Paddy, who quickly filled me in. He's a really entertaining guy. He said your test recording was great. Gardiner was very impressed."

"So it seems." Casey nodded, wishing she was in her smart outfit instead of the towelling robe. "I'm practically signed up. I'll get Adam Maynard to check everything out."

"Good idea. Lawyers take the time to read the fine print. Why didn't you tell me you were off to Sydney?" he asked. "I flew Dad and Leah in. There was plenty of room for you."

She shrugged. "I didn't want to bother you. Plus

I don't think your dad would have liked it. Isn't Sandra Gordon a favourite of his?"

"She must be." He grinned. "He's been nagging me to marry her for years."

"Look, let me throw some clothes on," she said, those golden eyes on her exquisite torture.

"Why don't you do it right here?" he suggested, his eyes full of mockery and mischief.

"Funny, Connellan." She might as well have shed the robe, so conscious was she of her naked body beneath.

Troy picked up on her thoughts as though she had spoken them aloud. "Actually what I came to ask is, will you have dinner with me? Hamburger and fries or something? Of course if you need to wear something you've just bought—" he glanced over at a stack of smart shopping bags bearing top labels "—we could try one of the top restaurants?"

"It *must* be a top restaurant," she said firmly, deciding she wanted to look beautiful for him.

"Then I'll see if I can get a booking at the best there is. Seven-thirty suit you? I'll pick you up here."

She tried not to show her wild anticipation. "I'm looking forward to it."

"Me, too, McGuire." He stood up, a superb hunk of a man in a caramel coloured suit, blue and white striped shirt, dark blue silk tie with a gold stripe. His hair she noticed had been recently cut but not even the hairdresser had wanted to take too much off that tawny bronze mane. It still kicked up off his nape. "I'd best be going. I have to report to my old man."

"How are things between you?" she asked.

He shrugged. "Nothing much changes."

"In sharp contrast to Leah? She told me your father was buying her a city apartment?"

"So he is but Dad and I will get to use it from time to time."

"And she didn't get to tell you I was in this hotel, either?"

"Come on, Casey," he lightly jeered. "You know Leah's current deepest, darkest fear is I'll fall madly in love with you."

She laughed out loud. "Well have you or not?"

"Let's start with the easy stuff," he suggested. "Is there an attraction? You bet there is." He headed towards the door with his silent big-cat tread, but at the last moment shot out an arm and pulled her to him. "I've missed you."

"I've missed *you!*" It was on Casey's lips to say, *I love you,* but she swallowed the words. Loving went hand in hand with the potential for pain.

"I hope so," he said and dropped a brief kiss on her mouth that had her yearning for more. "You can tell me all about this afternoon over dinner. Right now I'd better check in with Dad."

"Want to tell him you're having dinner with Jock McIvor's big surprise daughter?"

"Absolutely not. It's none of his business."

Casey was just as certain his sister and his dad, who didn't sound like a lot of fun, wouldn't agree. Wouldn't it be an awful, terrible thing for Troy Connellan, who it appeared was Outback aristocracy, to get tangled up with a girl very definitely from the wrong side of the tracks. Her half sisters, Darcy and Courtney were one thing. They were the McIvor heiresses. She was the daughter of a woman, an adulteress, who had overdosed on drugs.

Casey had the sinking feeling she would never live down the social stigma of her past. It was a very comforting feeling to know she had money. They had all agreed on a settlement she privately thought mind blowing. Maybe respectability was beyond her. She was one of those who through no fault of their own had ugly dark places in her life.

CHAPTER SEVEN

HE TOOK her to a beautiful restaurant with Harbour
views, owned and run by a woman, a great restau-
rateur and author with an international reputation.

The restaurant, predictably, was filled with a mix
of formally dressed people and smart casual—a
jacket for the men was obligatory—who all looked
very happy to be there. The dining rooms were
lovely: glass walls, glittering harbour lights, shimmering silver and crystal, candles, flowers, elegant
without being opulent, luxuriant with magnificent
potted plants, the lighting very flattering, the wait-
ers all young and handsome, darkly Mediterranean.
She and Troy must have looked an eye-catching
pair because Casey intercepted both frankly open
and fairly discreet stares.

Being Sydney, they chose seafood, arguably the
best in the world, for starters. Seared freshly
shucked scallops with white truffle butter, served
with fettucini as a garnish. Casey hesitated over

succulent lobster, but finally settled on a lovely rich peppered duck breast with poached balsamic figs and crisps. Troy ordered char sui pork with a selection of Asian vegetables, all beautifully presented.

It was all so delightful Casey wondered when reality was going to hit.

They talked about many things, light, relaxing things to compliment the delicious meal. Casey relayed all the events of her afternoon, painting little cameos of the musicians who had backed her. Impromptu, effortless. Her soaring exhilaration at their skill, lifting her own performance to the heavens. He laughed at her stories. She laughed at his. Troy was, without doubt, entertaining company. And fate had thrown them together.

His burnished eyes caressed her while his generous mouth smiled. He'd told her in a number of different ways how beautiful she looked. Which ever way he put it, it sounded just right. Never a false note. He was absolutely brilliant at making her feel special. That perhaps more than his incredible sexiness was what she liked most about him. He made her feel she and her opinions were important to him. She'd had precious little of that, although she'd experienced plenty of lust, she'd taken bitter pleasure in scorning. She had an idea of herself that involved integrity.

Both of them bypassed dessert though glancing around at the other tables what the other diners were savouring looked luscious. Instead they shared a cheese platter and short black coffees.

Troy signalled for the bill. "What about a stroll around the waterfront?" he suggested. "We can take a cab or walk back to the hotel."

"A walk would be fine." She never wanted this enchanted evening to end.

They were on their way out hand in hand as a small party of late diners came in.

Chance, Casey reflected, fixing a smile on her face. Bloody rotten chance. She couldn't lose it. It just followed her around. Everything had been going so marvellously she'd felt she was walking on air.

Now this! But fronting up to bad situations was what she did best. At least the tiny, delicate-looking much older woman looked a real lady.

"My, my, so this is the friend you were talking about?" Paddy twinkled, his eyes moving over Casey with great pleasure. He'd heard enough from Leah to know Casey's background was the sticks. "Dirt poor! Very rough childhood, you know." Breeding counted. Casey looked a million dollars in a canary yellow silk and chiffon number decorated with swirls of gold sequins. The dress was cut like a slip with a marvellous chunk of costume jewellery around her neck and wrist only a tall, stunning woman could carry off. Beside her Leah wouldn't get a look in.

Never stand next to a goddess, Paddy thought, suddenly confronting the fact it was high time he and Leah broke up.

Troy, for his part, though he felt a stab of dismay mixed with extreme irritation—he figured Leah had something to do with this—made the introductions smoothly. His father had an old family friend on his arm, Madelyn Curtis, widow of the late Sir Geoffrey Curtis, the career diplomat.

Lady Curtis looked genuinely delighted, her still beautiful dark eyes sparkling up at Troy as if to say, "You naughty boy! Why have you hidden this glorious creature?"

Clifford Connellan on the other hand stopped short when he saw them. The expression on his face was a good indication he didn't approve of surprises sprung on him. He studied Casey as though she were the classic example of young woman he least wanted his son to get mixed up with.

"How do you do?" Very correct and formal. Tall, silver hair, patrician features, glinting gaze he had passed on to his daughter. "I hope they're right about this place, Troy," he said as though he couldn't imagine it could come up to his expectations. "We've had to wait to get in."

Shock, horror, the pain of it, to have to wait! Casey felt something inside her recoil from the old money elitist arrogance.

"The food's wonderful, Dad," Troy said, patiently, wondering why his father had to act the way he did. Over the years he'd turned into a regular pain in the ass.

"Had we known you intended dining here you and your friend—" another glinting glance at Casey "—could have joined us." Clifford Connellan's brows arched as if to say, "Why wasn't I informed?"

Lady Curtis hooted gently. "And spoil the fun? Come on, Cliff, these two young people want to be together. A pleasure to meet you, Casey," she said as the maître d who had been hovering came towards them. "Lovely to see you again, Troy. You're my very favourite godchild."

She lifted a tiny hand to pat Troy's cheek and he bent to kiss her. "I'll catch up with you, Mabs, before I go back."

"I'd like that, dear."

"Bye," Paddy called, playing the flute with his fingers.

Apparently they didn't deserve a friendly farewell from Clifford Connellan or his only daughter who merely nodded. Casey had caught Leah gaping at her dress, then her stilettos. For God's sake, isn't she *tall* enough? was written all over Leah's expression.

* * *

"I must apologise for my family," Troy said, when they were out in the street. He took her arm, tucking it through his.

"Obviously they were delighted to meet me," Casey said sarcastically.

"Don't worry about it." Troy felt very angry as well as embarrassed. "You're so *different* to what they're used to."

"Different to Sandra, you mean?" She pulled away from him slightly.

He drew her back. "I've told you, Casey, Sandra is just a friend. I've known her all my life. I was never in love with her. I never will be. End of story."

"Tell your dad that. Turns out he's a nice guy."

"Let's leave Dad out of it," Troy groaned. "I won't let them spoil our night."

"Hell, I thought they did a good job."

"Casey...*pleeze!*"

"Do you think your sister had anything to do with their choice of venue?"

Another groan. "Leah's long been in training as a spy. Mostly for my dad. But no way do they run my life. No way would I allow them to influence my choice of bride. Let alone make that choice. Why do you think I'm constantly at loggerheads with my father? His idea of the perfect son is someone who does exactly what he's told. That's never me. I'd give up my heritage before I'd commit to that."

Casey was outraged on his account. "I can't believe you'd be forced into such a thing?"

"I don't know," he said. "Dad pushes me to the limit. I take off. He backs off. The truth of it is he needs me. Vulcan needs me. I know what I'm doing. The men work well under me. They give me one hundred per cent. Stuff like that. It's important out here to have trust and loyalty. To treat all the people working for us fairly."

"You'd do that," she said, nodding her firm approval. "At least that's the way I see you. A straight shooter."

"Who finally might have to make another life for himself."

"Could you? Would you?" She glanced at his strong rugged profile.

"Both." His fingers tightened on her. "I have money my mother left me. Not a fortune but enough to get me started. That's the only thing that keeps Dad in line. The money my mother left me. Hard work would eventually get me what I want."

"But what you really want is your family heritage?"

He sighed. "Nothing is certain in life, Casey. You know that. From what you've been telling me you have a career ahead of you. A big career by the sounds of it. You have everything going for you."

"Everything?" She gave a little smile. "I don't *only* want a career, Troy. I want family. My family. My children. Lots of them. I swear I'll know how to treat them."

"Well that's wonderful!" He gave her a white grin. "But, hey, don't you want a husband somewhere in there?"

"I don't know," she said soberly. Rule One. Men weren't to be trusted.

"That's a bit silly. Are you saying you're considering going along to a sperm bank?"

"Don't be ridiculous, Connellan," she snapped.

"Come on now. Be happy," he cajoled her in a deep sexy voice. "Personally I don't see why you can't have both. A career and a husband. Call me old-fashioned—"

"You *are!*" she jibed.

"No, Casey, I'm not and you know it. I wouldn't object to a trial marriage."

She felt her heart bound in her breast. "What are you talking about?" She knew she sounded flustered but it couldn't be helped.

"We're speaking hypothetically, aren't we?" he asked in a smooth voice.

"Sure." Her heart quietened. She never knew where this guy was leading her.

"I don't know much about the music business," Troy said earnestly, "but it seems to me a married woman could find time to have kids, cut CD's and make videos? You could write your beautiful songs anywhere. Pour out your sad heart. You could even fit in a few judicious personal appearances."

"Got it all figured out, have you?"

He leaned sideways and kissed her temple. "I care about you, McGuire," he said. "I really do."

In the elevator they stood alone, staring at each other. "I want you," he said, gleaming eyes mesmeric. "I want you very much."

"How would you feel if your dad and Leah knocked on the door?"

"Obviously we'd put a Do Not Disturb notice on the door."

"*You* didn't take any notice of it," she reminded him. "Just the thought of your father demanding to be let in, is death to romance."

"Is that so?" His golden eyes moved briefly, very powerfully over her.

They couldn't even wait until the door was closed behind them before they started into kissing. She was eager, hungry for him, sexually aroused all evening. She had never experienced such urgency for a man. It was like a raging torrent sweeping her headlong downstream. Arms and legs locked, they explored each other's mouth, fiercely, gently, voluptuously, tenderly, then starting the cycle all over again, overlapping one into the other.

"You're beautiful, so beautiful!" he muttered. "I can't get enough of you, McGuire," he groaned in frustration. "Can we get this dress off before I tear it?"

"I'll help." She was gasping for breath, as delirious as he was to explore their sexuality. If they only had this one night she thought she might be able to live on it for the rest of her life.

Swiftly she found the zipper, pulled it so her dress parted and slithered down to the carpet. The dress that had cost a fortune. She stepped out of it and he caught it up, placing it carefully over a chair. Rare for a man to be so *gentle, so considerate.*

"Oh my God!" He turned back, his breath almost stopped in his throat. She had left both bedside lamps on when she went out, now he saw her standing before him in her champagne coloured bra and bikini briefs, her flawless white skin, in striking contrast to the fire of her hair. It tumbled around her shoulders, framing her face. Her white breasts were perfect. How his hands ached to cup them; to tease the deep pink nipples with his teeth. Her eyes, staring back at him, were the most brilliant blue he had ever seen. She was a *glorious* woman. She bewitched him. He wanted her more than he had ever wanted anything in his life.

Casey registered the tautening of his strongly

hewn features, the hunger that prowled in his eyes. Because of the circumstances of her life she had never really trusted any man. But she trusted Connellan. Was that the way it was? You trusted a man even when you shouldn't?

She took a step towards him still wearing her gold stilettos. "Take off your jacket," she ordered breathlessly, unable to resist him. "I can last long enough to help you. The shirt, the tie—I *love* that tie—and the pants." Her hands were already on him, eager, super efficient even under the pressure of arousal. Pleasure kept rising. And rising. A wonderful masculine scent was coming off his body, enhancing the ecstasy. It made her senses spin.

His skin was velvet to her satin. She clenched her fingers on the bronze pelt on his broad chest, thrilled by his wonderful physique. She saw something else. He was dark gold all over and powerfully aroused.

And so they were naked, the two of them wrapped in radiant heat, each making soft incoherent sounds at the bliss of body to body, female to male, skin on skin.

"Casey!" Her name was a husky exclamation.

He could feel the violent beat of his own blood that had gathered in his groin. He reached back blindly to strip off the quilt then in a swift motion he lifted her in his arms. Her weight seemed to him insubstantial. She was all silky flesh and long del-icate bones. He debated removing those sexy stilet-tos but after a moment did.

"I like every single thing about you," he said, a golden blaze in his eyes.

"Tell me how much you want me?"

"I'm going to show you," he said. "That's even better."

With a feeling of incredible elation like something out of a dream, he watched as she lifted her beauti-ful body to him, arching her back, straining, demand-ing, asserting her overwhelming desire for him.

It was all that Troy needed.

He covered her like an enveloping rug, bracing his strong arms on either side of her, taking his weight. She was shuddering sweetly beneath him, her body moving in anticipation of his entry. She was ready, aligning herself, but he held back with exquisite deliberation. What was passing between them was pure ecstasy.

At just the right moment, as she opened herself beneath him, he was inside her, plunging slowly, deeply, lifting her firm buttocks higher, feeling those magnificent long legs grip his sides.

The act of taking her had a purity and a rightness about it. He felt a great rush of gratitude, too, as though he had been granted a precious gift. This was the one woman he wanted to make his own. He knew it in his heart, in his mind, in his body.

He could feel the first rippling contractions in her body start up and intensify so her whole body was left quivering. He registered her soft moans, her tossing head, silky hair flying everywhere, covering her face. Then he abandoned himself to the ecstasy that was of a magnitude he had never known. Shafts of white lightning were burying themselves deep within his body. His muscles were knotted with acute tension like some sleek powerful big cat. He wanted her to feel what he was feeling only his need was so great he didn't think he could control it much longer. If only she loved him as he knew he loved her! If only they could spend their lives together! She wanted children. What a great blessing it would be if they were *his* children. He had to do whatever he could to make her see she needed *him* as much as a career. Not that he could deny her wonderful talent.

"My beautiful Casey," he whispered. "I'm not hurting you am I?" Tall as she was, compared to him her woman's body was almost fragile.

She clung to him, pressing her mouth to his shoulder. "No, I love it." It was so *true!* Love flooding her. She understood it, though she couldn't yet speak it. The doors of heaven had never been opened to *her.*

He rocked into her. Infinitely tender. Deep, deeper, sensuous rhythms she was matching. Finally when he thought he could hold out no longer she called out his name.

It sounded so strange. The sort of cry that would haunt his heart. It was the tremulous heartfelt outpouring of a young girl. As though her innocence had come back to her.

It sent him tumbling right over the edge into roaring, rapturous oblivion.

Afterwards still wrapped together, still overwhelmed by the magic they had made together they began to share their most private thoughts. Memories of the past both of them had made sure they kept to themselves.

Now the flood gates were open.

Casey spoke about her early life with her mother. Her mother's vulnerabilities she thought she couldn't rise above without the help of first alcohol, then drugs. Casey spoke about that terrible day, the waking nightmare, of her mother's death, aware Troy was trying to soothe her with his hands and the kisses he dropped on her temple, her cheek and her bare shoulder. She hadn't really intended to tell him much about The Home. But it came tumbling out as though she had waited for this *one* person to confide in.

"Casey." He wrapped her closer, appalled at the

terrible experiences she had lived through and survived. Not only survived she had emerged as someone quite special. Casey McGuire-McIvor had courage, integrity, a great fighting spirit, qualities that sat very well with him. Another child burdened by such a disastrous start might well have taken the downward road to self-destruction. Casey had definitely moved up.

If she had been willing to share her innermost thoughts and feelings with him Troy proved his trust in her by speaking of his own life.

He tucked one long arm behind his head. "So much of what we are comes from family. Family relationships. I guess most families carry the same baggage. Often through generations. In the case of migrants they probably carry them from country to country. My dad and I weren't always so polarized. We were friends. He took me everywhere with him. He loved me. He was proud of me."

"So how did it change?" Casey snuggled in to his warm body, marvelling at how *right* it seemed.

"My mother's death," he said. "Just like you and millions of others, it was a great turning point in my life. Mothers are very special people. Losing her affected not only my life, but Dad's life, too. Leah was broken-hearted, but that was when Dad let her in and shut me out. You saw tonight how closely Leah resembles Dad. I'm my mother's side of the family. I have a cousin, Elliot, who could be my double. Both of us have our unusual coloured eyes. My mother's eyes. Perhaps my father finds it difficult to look into them since he believed my mother was unfaithful to him."

A mystery solved. Casey remained silent, waiting for him to go on.

"Sometimes I think she must have been," he said with a sadness that gripped Casey as well. "Other times I give her the benefit of the doubt. I adored her. We were very close in the best and brightest way. My parents had a friend called Robert Sinclair, a writer and journalist. He was a widely travelled man. When he was home he often visited us. Leah and I called him Uncle Robert which pretty well reflects what we all thought about him. He was a man's man, at home with my father out on the station, but he was a woman's man as well. A sensitive man. A lover of beauty in all its forms. I know he delighted in my mother's company.

"One afternoon when I was fourteen they went off riding together. It was a season when the tropical North had had torrential rain. Those floodwaters run into our Three Rivers System and from there into the maze of interlocking water channels that cover our part of the world. Tourists have camped in dry creek beds only to be washed away in our flash floods. Uncle Robert and my mother should have known better."

"How did it happen?" Casey asked quietly, the tension in his body communicating itself to her.

"No one could come up with a satisfactory answer. The horses came home. They didn't. They were found two days later. Locked in each other's arms. Not even the raging flood could separate them."

"But he would have been trying with all his might to protect her?" Casey reasoned, lifting her head to stare into his face.

"Of course." He nodded. "It's what any man would do. Only my father said afterwards Uncle Robert had been in love with her. I don't think he would have said it only he was under a great deal of emotional pressure. He said, too, he'd spoken to my mother about it, but she denied there was anything between them but friendship. Apparently my father wanted Uncle Robert's visits to stop. He thought them too painful, too dangerous. Maybe Uncle Robert and my mother were so engrossed in breaking up they didn't exercise their normal caution. We'll never know. I know my father was desperately upset. Truly grief stricken. He changed after that. All the lightness of heart went out of him. The humour. The biggest change was towards me. He turned away from me as though I was somehow responsible. Betrayed his trust passing messages between the two of them or something. Having prior knowledge. Of course I didn't."

"But there could have been nothing in it, Troy," Casey insisted. "Even if this Uncle Robert had worshipped your mother, it doesn't mean she was unfaithful. She was a married woman with two children. She must have loved your father to marry him? Why would she want to jeopardize her marriage and perhaps lose custody of her kids?"

"Passion makes fools of us all," he sighed. For a long time he had persecuted himself with the idea his mother had fallen out of love with his father.

"Surely we've just experienced passion?" she countered sitting up and leaning over him. "Are you saying our coming together like this was a mistake?"

"It's the best thing that's ever happened to me," he said.

"Right answer." She subsided with a great sigh of relief onto his broad chest. "Well then, be kinder to yourself and your mother. All we can do, Troy, is move on."

CHAPTER EIGHT

GLENN GARDINER lost no time promoting his new client. Over two days of intensive work and concentration Casey cut her first album which Gardiner was certain was going to make her reputation. Some of the songs were familiar territory to country fans, but delivered in Casey's own highly distinctive style. There was no mistaking her for anyone else, Paddy said. Paddy was in on everything as though he had appointed himself her honorary agent. She sang slow songs. She sang fast. She sang rock, backed by a team of wonderful musicians on electric and acoustic guitar, drums and percussion, keyboards, trumpet, alto sax, tenor sax. In her own segment of six the songs that were closest to her, her own, she utilized a beautiful violin. She couldn't thank the band enough for the way they lifted her, every one of them putting their heart and soul into the performance.

Her own ballads, the sad songs, were full of the

naked vulnerability and the heart ache that had surrounded her for most of her life. With the violin playing counterpoint she accompanied herself on these, using a guitar Matt, the lead guitar, lent her. It was a vastly superior instrument to her own and she thrilled to it, bringing it to plangent life. Matt assured her she was a good guitarist, but he was willing to coach her if she wanted. She wanted. It was an honour! Matt was the best in the business.

Next came the video clip where movement had to be fitted to music. She had to learn dance steps. She had to learn to co-ordinate those steps with great trained dancers. She had to learn how to act. Apparently the way she *looked* was no problem. The camera seemed to love her. But those routines!

"Come on, Casey! Show us what you can do. Show us your heart. Show us your soul. Make with the feet!"

"Making with the feet" was the hardest part, but somehow she managed and for that a lot of the credit went to Courtney. Courtney had accompanied her to Sydney for which she was immensely grateful. Courtney, the ex-P.R. whiz kid looked after her, remarkably like a mother, making phone calls, fielding them, getting on with Gardiner famously which when it came down to business was quite a feat, looking after costumes, getting her to appointments on time, helping her with those dance steps. Courtney was a beautiful natural dancer. She gave herself up to it the way Casey gave herself up to her songs. As it turned out, Courtney was also a very good teacher licking her pupil into shape.

Marian and her husband Peter wouldn't hear of the girls staying at an hotel. They had a lovely home with plenty of room and it gave Courtney an opportunity to be with her mother.

Crossing George Street on her way back to her car, Courtney was stunned to see Adam walking the opposite way with the lights. She blinked hard. Maybe it was wishful thinking. It wasn't. It was Adam, and he looked so handsome, so confident to the core, so professional in his beautifully tailored dark suit, she felt herself choke up. What was he doing here? Business, of course. He was carrying a leather briefcase.

She put out her hand. He hadn't seen her, obviously preoccupied. "Adam!" She didn't know if he heard her, her voice was so soft.

"Courtney, I didn't know you were here." He stopped in his tracks, his brilliant eyes whipped over her with such intensity it threw her even more off-balance. His arm locked tight around her as he led her safely to the pavement. She might have been a piece of porcelain or a precious child. "What *are* you doing here?"

She saw delight he couldn't hide burn in his eyes.

'I'm with Casey." She looked up at him, realizing how terribly she had missed him, despite their inevitable confrontations. "We're staying at my mother's. Casey has cut her first album and a video clip. She's on her way."

"That's marvellous! If anyone needs a lucky break it's Casey." He steered them into a quiet corner away from the surging crowd. "Not that luck has all that much to do with it. She has a real gift."

"Yes she has. The album goes on sale at the end of the month. We don't know yet about the video clip. She looks and sounds sensational. I'm so proud of her."

"I can see that." When she spoke of her half sister, her expression was illuminated with the love and pride that flowed through her. It was not at all the troubled look he had encountered. Of course they hadn't parted on the best of terms, something for which he cursed himself. If anyone was to blame it was he. This young woman couldn't do anything that smacked of duplicity and greed. He was crazy to have doubted her for a moment. She was as lovely as she looked.

"What are *you* doing in Sydney?" she asked, pulses hammering just to be with him. "Business?"

He nodded. "The usual. I'm here until tomorrow." He shot up a spotless white cuff, checking his watch. "Please don't tell me you're doing anything tonight?"

She found herself caught in his dark probing gaze. "There's some party on."

"There's always a party on. Are you sure you want to go to it?" he asked sardonically.

She was silent for a little minute. "I have to make an appearance. The party's for Casey. Glenn wants to show her off. What did you have in mind?"

"Just being together," he murmured. "Living dangerously." His lips curved in a smile.

"You could come to the party for a while. We could leave early? It would be fine with Casey. She's the one in the spotlight. Everyone wants to meet her. The word has gone out."

"So a late supper?" he suggested. "Unfortunately I have to rush now," he said apologetically. "I'm never late for an appointment if I can help it."

"Don't let me keep you." She touched his arm. "Where do we meet?"

"I'll pick you up at your mother's," he said, turning his head, checking on the lights. "I know her address. We keep in touch."

"You *do?*" Her eyebrows shot up in astonishment. She doubted if he even heard her. He was already stepping off smartly at the crossing, leaving Courtney coming up for air.

Her mother had never breathed a word.

* * *

The party was already underway by the time they arrived. Casey, looking drop dead glamorous in a vivid amethyst silk halter necked dress she and Courtney had picked out, broke free of an admiring group to greet them.

She kissed Courtney, studied Adam with approval. "It's good to see you, Adam!" Her sister had very good taste. "Now come along you two." She took them arm in arm. "I want you to meet our hostess. She's quite a character. Isn't this the most wonderful house!"

It certainly was. Not everyone got to live right on Sydney Harbour. Their hostess turned out to be Mrs. Pandora Featherstone, who was quite familiar to Courtney and Adam through her long, well documented social life. Pandora enjoyed great social clout in both Sydney and Melbourne, a platinum haired septuagenarian who, thanks to a Los Angeles cosmetic surgeon, looked twenty years younger, in flamingo-pink and a queen's ransom in South Sea pearls and diamonds. She made a beeline for them while all around her people fell back like the parting of the Red Sea. It was the high class Pandora Glenn Gardiner had persuaded to throw Casey's launch party. No one better!

The guests were a very heady mix of show business people, the cream of the socialites, people from the art world, business tycoons and a sprinkling of politicians. The women had really let their hair down with their dressing. So much to admire! The men as usual were far more conservative; black tie, a sprinkling of gorgeous bow ties, silk ties, expensive lounge suits. Notable exceptions stood out. The arty types, mostly the musicians—one in tight bell bottomed cyclamen satin trousers and sequinned shirt—who later on in the evening kept the music pumping.

All of a sudden Casey was *someone*. Courtney found herself left wondering rather sadly if Troy Connellan had got his fingers badly burned.

They stayed longer than they intended, waiting until after Casey had sung a bracket of songs backed by the well known musician Matt Langford who seemed to have taken her under his wing. It was quite something to see a houseful of carousing guests—the champagne flowed like water—fall silent after the first few notes that issued from Casey's mouth, rich, melodious, powerfully stirring. The only upset of the evening as far as Adam was concerned was Paddy Nicholls's infuriating attempts to start a fling with Courtney who looked exquisite in one of her luminous chiffon dresses that made her look like a ray of light. And Paddy wasn't the only guy who couldn't tear his eyes off her. It got to the stage Adam started to think he couldn't take much more of it. He wanted Courtney to himself. He was madly in love with her. So much so he'd completely missed all the lustful glances aimed in his direction.

They took a cab back into the city, stopping off at a little Italian bistro famous for its barista who prided himself on the perfection of his coffee.

"Will you have something with that?" Adam asked, after she ordered a long black.

"Yes, please. Something chocolate." Although there was enough food at the party to feed a third world country, she'd found herself unable to unwind enough to eat. Paddy Nicholls's attentions for one thing had bothered her. Paddy was nice but he couldn't wipe the cash registers out of his eyes. Besides she felt committed to *one* man. That alone had her worried some predatory female would take Adam off her. There were hordes of them on the prowl. All good-looking. All sexy. All eyeing him off. Jealousy was just so primitive. It had killed her appetite.

Now she had Adam to herself and it was *brilliant!*

"Chocolate as in cheese cake, mud cake, decadent chocolate cake, chocolate torte, chocolate truffles?" he was asking, glancing over at the glass display cases filled with mouth-watering confections.

"Why not the decadent chocolate cake? I can handle it."

"Are you feeling decadent?" He smiled at her, as though more seductive things were in store.

"Of course not!" she said piously, not ready for a lie detector test.

"What a shame. I thought you might like to come back with me to the firm's apartment where I'm staying."

She felt a delicious thrill not unlike a small electric shock. "Not an hotel?"

"Not for years. The firm does so much business here they've found it cheaper to maintain an apartment. It's available to all of us, all the year round. It just so happens I have it to myself at the moment."

Her lips curved into a teasing smile. "And you think I might be tempted to join you there?"

"I'm hoping and praying you will." Intensity was back in his dark eyes. "I'm in too deep. Aren't you?"

"Tough question." At the last moment she shied away from revealing her heart. "Maybe what I'm feeling has more to do with your sex appeal than your analytical legal mind."

Of course it was a little dig. "Please add to that my advocacy skills of persuasion." He leaned towards her, his chiselled mouth faintly twisted. "It's not the big seduction scene, Courtney. Just the chance at a little privacy. Here comes the waiter. Two long blacks, two decadent chocolate cakes. That's it?"

Her laugh was light and lovely. "If I need to have another piece I'll let you know."

The firm's Potts Point apartment was a bit like a prosperous men's club, Courtney thought. Black granite floored entry, ivory and chocolate coloured walls, a step up to the kitchen, dining, living area. The dark stained polished floors were covered here and there with taupe rugs. In the sitting area a rich cocoa-brown leather sofa and two deep comfortable armchairs were arranged around a large square dark timber coffee table. Sliding glass doors gave onto a deck that looked east and west to the night time glitter of the city.

"Do you want to see the bedroom. Just for fun?" he asked, his voice sardonic, his eyes a whole lot warmer. "Two bedrooms actually. Some of the partners like to travel with their wives."

"Perhaps you should consider getting married?" she suggested sweetly. "The big wigs at legal firms usually like commitment from their rising young partners." She followed him down the passageway.

The subdued colour scheme continued. No doubt to make the apartment seem more spacious than it was. Courtney peeked into the second bedroom, took longer inspecting the master bedroom. Three ebony framed oriental prints hung above the bed. The floor was carpeted in rich chocolate, the bed

spread combined with white linen was surprisingly
luxurious, quilted black and chocolate velvet.

"Very nice!" She gave her nod of approval. "Not
meant for the ladies but really very comfortable.
The Boys Own Club."

"It doesn't seem like that with you here with me."

Wanting him so badly she felt a contrary urge to
tease him some more. "I expect I'm not the first
woman you've brought here?" Without waiting for
him to answer she walked back along the passageway to the open plan living room, seating herself
on the sofa.

"No, just tiny, delicate little you." He gave her a
mocking smile, taking the armchair opposite her.
Against the rich dark leather she shimmered. Her
hair in the lamplight molten gold, a veil of gold lace
over her pale silk dress, gold evening sandals. An
angel who could inflame.

"Is that the truth?" Her blue eyes searched his.

"I wouldn't lie to you, Courtney."

"No, you don't like lies."

She seemed to withdraw a little and he didn't
want that to happen. "By the way, I've been meaning to tell you, I ran into your ex-boss recently,
Helen Taubman."

"Really!" Her expression lightened. "Where
was this?"

"Actually I've seen her at functions any number

of times, but we were never introduced. It was a Government House cocktail party. A mutual friend introduced us. She knew of my connection with you, the legal side anyway, and we got to talking. She sends her love. She told me how much she misses having you around. You were absolutely the 'tops' with her." In fact Ms Taubman had as good as raved about her ex-number one assistant, painting a picture of Courtney wildly at odds with the picture that awful bitch Barbra had tried hard to present.

"She was a great boss." Courtney smiled. "I loved working for her."

"No misgivings?" he asked, seriously.

"Not at all. I'm finding my new life much more rewarding."

"So what are you going to do when Darcy marries? It's not long now."

"No." There was excitement and a touch of sadness in her tone. "Time goes so fast but I suspect not fast enough for Darcy and Curt. As for me, I'm going to find myself a good husband," she announced. "I don't know who it is yet."

"Just remember he has to get past me. No fortune hunters," he said bluntly.

"I thought you were never going to mention Paddy." Her lovely mouth curved into a wide smile. "I think he's got me in his sights."

"You mean he's finished with Leah?" he asked sarcastically.

"I seem to have pushed Leah right out of the picture. Of all the men I've known *you* are actually the only one I've considered. But then, there are far too many barriers."

"Such as?"

"We have different lives. You have your career. I have Murraree. Anyway, what's your star sign? I'm sure we're incompatible."

"Except when we make love." He stood up, moving his lithe elegant body towards her, smooth, controlled, purposeful.

The room seemed to swirl around her. "I didn't say you could join me." She tipped her blonde head back against the plush leather to study him.

"It's more romantic the two of us on the sofa surely?" He fetched up a taut smile.

Colour flooded her cheeks. "There's some change in you, Adam, what is it?"

"I'd change everything about myself to get you," he muttered, not sitting beside her as she thought he intended, but doing what he most liked, lifting her with great ease across his knees, close to his heart. There she seemed to melt, her shining head flung back against his arm, the neckline of her gossamer dress dipping so he could see the upper slopes of her small breasts, as pretty as cream roses.

"I thought you didn't like me?" She searched his dark handsome face, aware there was some healing in him.

"The fact is I fell in love with you. On sight," he told her tautly, holding off the moment when her soft tender mouth would be under his.

"Ah, is that why you were so *hard* on me?" she asked carefully.

"Forgive me, Courtney." Very gently he smoothed back her silky halo of curls. "You can't imagine how hard I was on myself. We all throw up smoke screens to hide ourselves from hurt. I did that better than most. I know better now."

"I'm sorry, too," she said quietly.

"Whatever for? You've got nothing to be sorry for."

"It's just that I—" She dragged in a little breath ready to confess her own spirited efforts to discomfort him.

Only he said, "Don't talk." His brilliant dark eyes betrayed his driving needs. It wasn't talk he needed.

"No." The realization she was discovering true happiness began to hum inside her. There was nothing more she wanted in the world but to share it.

"I love you," she said. It wasn't forced out of her. It flowed as naturally as a bubbling spring.

For a long heartbeat he stared back, as though he couldn't quite take it in. "Oh, Courtney," he groaned. "I don't deserve you."

She lifted her arms to encircle his neck, a lovely bloom of colour in her cheeks. "You can soon rectify that. Tell me, if you had to choose me or your career what would the answer be?"

He read the intensity in her eyes, as clear and blue as the sky. "Look at it this way." The desire he felt for her was making his voice uncharacteristically gritty. "I'm not addicted to my career, but I am, however, addicted to *you*. You've stolen my heart. As for you? Could you leave Murraree to come to me?"

She was surprised to feel tears well into her eyes. It was evident from his expression she was meant to take his question very seriously. She drew a deep breath, the speed with which things were happening making her heart flutter. "If it meant losing you otherwise the answer is an unequivocal yes."

Elation surged through him. It was so dazzling so transforming, he could have shouted aloud "Then we have to come up with a solution, don' we?" he said, his voice suddenly full of hope. "O course you would need to marry me?"

Now the tears truly spilled onto her cheek. "I'n awake, aren't I?" she asked softly. "I'm no dreaming?"

"Courtney, sweetheart." He bent his dark head taking the teardrops into his mouth like champagne "You give me light and love. You can't know wha that means to me. Ever since I lost my parents, de spite all the love my grandparents gave me, I've lived in a world that often seemed full of shadows and tragic memories. Ever since I met you I've come to realize the shadows have gradually shifted away. At first I couldn't believe such a beautiful creature had come into my life. There had to be some catch. I'd learned the hard way life is so unfair. Now I feel I'm standing in the sunshine, revelling in your brightness. Am I making any sense?" He felt like pouring out his soul to her.

Radiance lay on her, like a very special magic. "Perfect sense, my love." Her tone was ineffably tender.

"Thank God!" he answered with a great rush of gratitude. Heaven had sent him an angel. He lifted her closer to his heart, his mouth coming down on hers, warm, hungry, reverent, yet caressing all the senses.

His breath was scented with chocolate and coffee.

It might have been the most powerful aphrodisiac in the world, so passionate was her response.

Love is a blessed thing. For Adam it offered deliverance from his tragic past. It offered a joy and a harmony he had never known.

For Courtney it was finding her *true* home.

Marian was ecstatic when Adam called next day with an arm full of fragrant pink roses to go through the charming motions of asking for Courtney's hand in marriage.

Marian laughed and she cried.

"Isn't that wonderful! So wonderful! I know you'll be good to her."

"Better than good, Marian," Adam assured her. "Most wonderfully good. I don't think I deserve her."

Courtney clung to him, thrilled by his open heart-edness. Happiness blazed in her blue eyes. All her uncertainties had been swept away. Today began a new life.

Marian knew these two truly loved each other. She had taken to Adam on sight, over time growing quite fond of him. She knew he was clever and strong. She knew he would love, honour and protect her daughter as Courtney's father never had her.

Happy with her second husband, Peter, Marian had never forgotten the painful years of her first marriage, the unpleasantness and the disgrace of Jock McIvor's numerous affairs. The cost had been high. All three of his daughters had suffered. None more so than Casey.

Marian had had her suspicions Jock was mixed up with someone when she was carrying Courtney. Incredible after so much time had passed the result of that dangerous liaison, Casey, had come into their lives. Marian was enormously grateful the family situation couldn't have turned out better when it so easily could have gone disastrously wrong. The sisters had bonded before they had ever dealt with the past. They were *blood* and blood truly was thicker than water.

Marian who was slightly in awe of Casey—she had so much of Jock's aura—was gradually growing closer to her which was what they both wanted. Beautiful Darcy who was to be married very soon had allowed her grateful mother back in to the charmed circle. The pain of what had happened would never go away. Marian knew that. But time was a great healer.

She would never have gotten away from Jock in the first place, only she knew about some of the secret deals, one in particular, he had clinched. She had made it her business to find out when she finally decided she had to leave him. Even now she recalled with a shudder how she had screwed up her nerve, raiding his safe in search of documents. Of course he thought she was too feather-brained to remember the combination. But one time, after a function on the station, when he was putting her jewellery away, he had made what amounted to a big mistake. He had allowed her to remain in his study, unmindful or uncaring of the fact she was staring intently over his shoulder.

Such carelessness from Jock! She had no difficulty remembering the combination. Why had she allowed him to treat her like a fool? Maybe if she'd been older when he married her. All the maybes!

The information she had gained, had won her her
freedom. Or freedom for her and Courtney. Not for
Darcy who had to remain behind with her father.
Damaging disclosures or not—only Marian knew
she would never have told, it was just a lever—
Jock would have killed her before he let Darcy go.
Jock had power. Lots of power.

Now Courtney and Adam wanted to be married.
The family had to celebrate Darcy's and Curt's marriage first. Such grace had come into their lives. It
had taken a long time but Marian knew the bad
times were behind them. Casey's feet were already
set on the road to success. Casey had Jock's powerful personality.

The one who was dearest and closest to Marian,
her lovely Courtney, her precious girl had a wonderful young man to claim her. Marian didn't know
why, but it suddenly struck her, if Adam could only
see himself in the role he'd be the ideal man to take
over the running of Murraree. Courtney would be
an enormous help to him there. They could work as
a team. In their conversations Adam had often remarked how much he loved Outback life. Of course
he had been reared on his grandfather's sheep and
cattle pastoral property. A miniature Murraree to be
sure, but Marian was certain Adam had the sterling
qualities to run a far bigger concern.

Ah well, it was for the young ones to decide. She

couldn't make their life decision, but she was thrilled with the turn of events. Courtney had chosen well. So had Darcy. Marian prayed when the time came Casey, too, would be blessed.

CHAPTER NINE

TROY halted work around two to return to the homestead to clean up a long gash in his arm. There wasn't much likelihood of its becoming infected. His tetanus shots were up to date, but rusty barbed wire required a little care. A length of it had spat back at him when he was inspecting some fencing that needed renewing.

It was intolerably hot but he never stopped. His father was doing less and less these days, leaving most things to him. He was beginning to wonder if his father had a health problem he wasn't saying anything about. Surely he'd tell Leah, even if he didn't want to discuss it with his son. It didn't seem right though. His dad was hale and hearty. He'd probably live to a ripe old age. His dad was king of the castle. He was the prince in waiting. Or was he?

When his dad came back from his trip to Darwin to see one of his mates he'd have to get his exact position clear. His long hard apprenticeship was over. He needed assurances he would inherit the station. It would have to be outright. It couldn't be broken up. No way was Leah suited for a life on the land. She took off every chance she got. Vulcan aside, Leah would still be left well-off. Their father spoiled her terribly.

He was cleaning up the wound in the first-aid room when Leah came to the door. "What happened?" she asked, real concern in her eyes.

"Nothing much." He gave her a smile. "A length of barbed wire attacked like a snake."

"It looks nasty." She frowned. Leah really loved her brother but she couldn't seem to show it. Sometimes she doubted her ability to show affection at all. Except to her father. Besides, she was hellishly jealous of the red-haired goddess who kept ringing trying to lure Troy to Sydney.

"Don't worry," he said calmly. "I've had my shots."

To her amazement Leah said what she was thinking, "You work awfully hard. How come Dad doesn't appreciate you like he should? I mean he couldn't do without you. You run the blasted place. As far as I can see the men answer to you."

Troy blew out a weary breath. "You know as well as I do, Leah, Dad and I have never been on real good terms for years now."

"You look so much like Mum that's why," Leah said, looking troubled. "I know she was a beautiful feminine woman and you're a great big hunk but you know what I mean. It's uncanny, the eyes."

Troy gave a thin smile. "Should that be a reason not to get on with your son? Your only son I might add."

"It's bloody sad," Leah announced after a pause. "I'm not sure anything can be done about it. In losing Mum we all got messed up. I've been given everything yet I still find life a struggle. Dad pampers me. Works you to death. Yet you're the pick of us. The best son in the world. Anyone else would be so *proud*. I'm not sure that he isn't, actually, but he's a bit like me or I'm a bit like him. We find it remarkably difficult to get things out. By the way, he's flying home this afternoon. That's what I came to tell you."

"Then I better get ready to lay my cards on the table," Troy said firmly because that was the way he was feeling. And then there was Casey!

She reacted to his determined expression. "I don't want Vulcan, Troy. Not even a half share. It's yours. What would I do with it? I don't give a damn about the place. That's awful I know, but it's the truth. I think Dad just likes to keep you on the hook. It's cruel really, and he's not cruel. Or not beyond repair. I think losing Mum desensitised him. Dad has had practically no contact with women, in the romantic sense I mean. The only one he really likes and trusts is Mabs."

"Yeah, well…" Troy shrugged. "Mabs has been

a widow for years and he hasn't rushed her to the altar. As for me, I've taken my lot like a dutiful son, but he's pushing me too far. I've been thinking seriously of striking out on my own."

"On your own?" Leah stared at him as if he'd expressed the need to reach the South Pole. "You've got to be kidding! Dad would be in shock. It hasn't got anything to do with Casey, has it? I know you're mad about her but she's got a big career ahead of her. No way she'd give it up."

"That remains to be seen," Troy said, his expression taut. "Why would she have to give it up anyway?"

"Are you *serious?*" Leah's good-looking face reflected her dismay. "You're in love with her, aren't you?"

Troy fixed his golden gaze on her. "Why sound so threatened? How many guys have you had and broken up with? I don't interfere in your affairs, Leah. Don't interfere in mine. When are you and Dad going to wake up to the fact Sandra means nothing to me beyond a friend. Give it up. It's a lost cause."

"So is Casey McIvor-McGuire, whatever her name is," Leah retorted. "She's got trouble written all over her. She's way too flamboyant to settle down on a cattle station. She's just using you Troy. Having some great sex, I bet. I've discussed this with Paddy. Everyone thinks she's going to be a big star. You want to get that clear, Troy. I don't want to see you get hurt. She'll dump you as soon as she's on her way. *Va...room!*" She imitated the sound of a speeding car. Then she half turned away. "Would you like a cup of tea?"

After that outburst Troy laughed. "Sure if you're making one." He ignored the throbbing in his arm. "And you're wrong about, Casey, Leah. She's too damned good for *me*."

Clifford Connellan had not arrived by late afternoon. They had confirmation from Planet Downs where he had stopped off on the way. That was around three. Uneasy Troy who had been keeping an eye on the sky, returned home, both he and Leah glued to the radio and the phone. Flying was a way of life in the Outback. Their father was a confident pilot with over thirty years of experience behind him. The Cessna was scrupulously serviced and maintained. There was some reasonable explanation. He had dropped in on their friends, the Ralstons, at Planet Downs. This was a trip he had made countless times before. It was highly unlikely he would make another stop. Nevertheless all attempts to contact him via radio frequency failed.

It was time to worry.

At first light the following morning a full scale air search was underway. Australia Search and Rescue as well as ten other aircraft piloted by Vulcan's neighbours retraced the flight path between Planet and Vulcan. Darcy, an experienced pilot, had joined the search as had her fiancé, Curt Berenger. Without the Cessna, Troy took the helicopter up with Leah as a spotter. Everyone was praying they would find the Cessna safely grounded, with Clifford Connellan walking out from under the wing to wave to his rescuers. It had happened many times before today.

But there was a time to be rescued and a time to die.

It was Darcy who first spotted the wreckage, a sweat breaking out on her body, a soft groan emerging from her throat. The Cessna had come down on hilly ground where the mirage shimmered and rose in quick silver whirlpools although the airspace around her had a crystalline quality. It looked bad. Like the plane had plummeted nose down from the sky. Parts of the aircraft were scattered over a wide area. No one could survive that.

It was difficult indeed to keep her voice under control as she relayed the news. The tears pouring down her face, Darcy kept circling until she sighted Vulcan's helicopter like some gigantic insect homing into the crash site directed by her port wingtip. She couldn't begin to gauge what Troy and Leah would be going through right now, looking down at the wreckage, knowing the body of their father lay somewhere in it. Landing for the helicopter wouldn't be a problem. Choppers could land almost anywhere.

There were other aircraft in the zone. Darcy banked away.

Soon the whole Outback would know of the tragedy. Accidents like this ravaged the entire Outback community where there was such a concentration of light aircraft.

Back in Sydney in Glenn Gardiner's office with its splendid view of Sydney Harbour Bridge Casey was reeling from the news of Troy's father's death and Glenn's opposition to her travelling to the Outback for the funeral.

"Be reasonable, Casey, you can't just up and go when there are so many things I have planned for you."

"I'm sorry, Glenn." After ten minutes of nonstop heavy persuasion Casey remained unmoved. "I must go. Troy Connellan is a good friend of mine."

"Friend? I thought he was a heck of a lot more?" Glenn was seriously worried. Romances had a way of sinking careers.

"I prefer not to talk about that right now, Glenn. Troy and Leah must be feeling absolutely wretched. The funeral is the day after tomorrow."

Glenn sighed. "Of course I understand, but it really does put things on hold. No chance Paddy could represent you? He's going."

"No way." Casey shook her head. "It's important for me to be there."

Glenn sighed again, under the circumstances trying to control his frustration. "Some of these meetings have taken weeks to set up but c'est la vie! In the midst of life we are in death as our old parish priest used to say. Just you take care of yourself, Casey. Any kind of aircraft isn't my favourite means of transport."

Henry Rutherford of Richards, Rutherford & Vine sat behind their father's desk ruffling through papers. It was the morning after the funeral and Leah was not feeling at all well. Grief had provoked her into drinking a bit too much, now she felt like throwing up. She was sick and apprehensive, too; their father might have carried out his random threats and rejected Troy's claim to taking over the station. It wasn't what she wanted. She was only too happy to relinquish any responsibility. If the worst came to the worst and Vulcan had been left to her, she would hand it over to Troy right away, though she had the dismal feeling he would be too proud to accept it. Troy just could walk right away from his birthright.

What was it that had caused the stressful situation

between Troy and their father? Leah agonised. It certainly wasn't Troy's fault. She had never found the courage to tackle her father about it. Instead she had ingratiated herself with him at every turn. Now she felt deeply ashamed. Time had come in her life for a change. She had to do something useful, even if she was a little confused what course that would take. Her father hadn't helped. He had pandered to her so much she had begun the long slip-slide into endless self-indulgence. It had to stop. It *would* stop.

Leah came back to the present.

"To simplify things," Henry Rutherford was saying ponderously, looking up at them over the top of his glasses. "Your father has left his estate divided into two. One part to each of you. Troy gets Vulcan and the out-stations. Leah you get the apartment in Sydney, and the beach house at the Gold Coast which by now is worth a small fortune. His portfolio will be split in two separate trust funds. Again one for each of you. I have been appointed trustee along with my partner, Raoul Vine. Each trust has equal proportions of blue chip stocks. I think you'll find they generate an extremely generous income each quarter. I've made a list of the companies. You can go through them carefully later. You'll be aware of them, Troy. You did so much business for your father.

"Under the terms of the trust you get the income

outright, Leah." He glanced into her white face. "Half of your income will be reinvested, half disbursed to you. After taxes it should amount to some $200,000 a year. That should keep you comfortably. All your late mother's jewellery is yours with the exception of your mother's sapphire and diamond engagement ring, a sapphire and diamond necklace with matching pendant earrings, all photographed, Connellan family heirlooms, which will go to Troy for his future bride. Or that is your father's earnest wish, Troy. There are generous bequests to charities, gifts to family friends." He handed over two thick folders full of documents. "These are your copies of all the legal material we've gathered at this stage of settlement. I know both of you will want to go over them."

Lady Curtis, Troy's godmother, who had come for the funeral and was staying with them at the homestead, insisted on taking the distraught Leah back to Sydney with her.

"I'll look after her, Troy," she assured him, her heart breaking at his expression.

"I know you will, Mabs." They were sitting on the front verandah, watching the imperial sun go down in splendour.

"Leah's life needs direction," Mabs said, turning her face to him. "Cliff, God rest him, spoilt her terribly. Leah has told me she wants to make a new start. I intend to help her. One has to give in this world. Not take."

"Anything you do is okay with me, Mabs," Troy said, comforted by her presence. "At least at the end Dad didn't cut me out."

Mabs looked astonished. "Surely you didn't think he would? I know nothing of this?"

"It doesn't matter now, Mabs," Troy said, easing back in his planter's chair. "Dad remembered I was his son."

"And who else would you be, pray?" Mabs's fine dark brows rose in amazement. "I remember when you were born. I remember your father's joy. I remember Elizabeth's beautiful Madonna face. They were ecstatic at your birth."

Troy gave a strangled laugh. "Things changed after we lost Mum."

"I know." Lady Curtis reached out to pat her much loved godson's hand. "Cliff was never the same again."

"Could you tell me something, Mabs?" Troy stared into her eyes. "Was Mum having an affair with Uncle Robert? You were around at the time. You and Mum were like sisters."

Mabs forced herself not to burst into tears. "Darling boy, your mother and I grew up together, Troy. We went to school and university together. We were forever in one another's homes. I was her chief bridesmaid. As for Rob?" Her dark eyes that had seen so much seemed to turn inwards. "He *was* in love with your mother. Who could blame him? Your mother cared for him. I know she did. Their personalities intermeshed so beautifully. But this is the *important* thing. The thing you have to grasp. Your mother would *never* have left your father. Much less you children. She took her marriage vows very seriously. She was a religious person. Remember I *knew* her. My own religious faith has helped me through life. Had Libby been thinking so radically I'm convinced she would have told me. She didn't. You know why? Her marriage was sacred. What happened was a terrible Act of God. Do you believe me?" She stared into his remarkable face.

"No one better to believe, Mabs." He tried to smile, failed.

"And what about that beautiful woman in your life, Casey? Now there's a very special person."

"No argument here." Now he did smile. "She's the woman I want, Mabs. Whether she wants me is another matter. She has a career now. She's taken off like I knew she would. I can't hold her back."

Mabs considered. "Of course you can't. But she dropped everything to be here for you, didn't she? I spoke to her after the funeral. You mean a great deal to her."

"Maybe her career will come to mean more?" He

shrugged. "She has a real gift, Mabs. You should
hear her."

"I intend to," Mabs said firmly. "I never figured
you for a quitter, Troy. If you want her and you
clearly do, go after her. Tell her how you feel. Don't
leave her in the dark. She's your dream. Don't let
your dream get away. If she truly loves you and you
love her you can find a way." She closed her eyes
for a moment, let out a sigh. "What woman doesn't
want a husband and children? Why should Casey
be any different? I had my dear husband but we
were never blessed with children. You're as close
as I came. Don't let Casey go back to Sydney without telling her how you feel. You could run the risk
of her going out of your life forever."

At Murraree Casey waited. The relationship she
and Troy had forged meant a great deal to her. She
had given him her body, shown him her soul. She
had flown to his side to give him support and comfort. She believed she had achieved both. Still she
waited when she knew she should be back in Sydney. Glenn Gardiner had already called her twice.
She understood where he was coming from, but he
wasn't going to run her life. Since she had lost her
mother and been sentenced to The Home she had
thought of herself as inconsolable. That she would
never get what she needed and wanted.

That wasn't the case. She had her sisters; utterly beautiful people, who had made her one of them though she had entered the picture as their father's love child. What a deep joy it was to her they had bonded. It hadn't been an on-going thing, slowly developing. It had happened that first day providing all three with a wonderful sense of abiding love. She was to be one of Darcy's bridesmaids, something that gave her enormous pleasure. Courtney very clearly had found her ideal man. Casey didn't want to be faced with the prospect of life without Troy Connellan in it.

What exactly did her career mean to her? Living most of her life with the *unhavable* could she really give up a career that was being handed to her on a silver platter? She didn't want to *abandon* it. That was true. Her music meant a lot to her. But she didn't want a career to be the sole focus of her life. After all she could still sing and write her songs without it. She had deep seated biological needs. She, the emotional orphan, wanted children. She wanted to be a warm, loving, nurturing mother. She wanted to fill a role her own poor little mother hadn't been able to fill. She wanted to get back *hope*.

All importantly, she wanted Troy Connellan to father her children. She had learned enough about him to know he'd do the job just fine. If only he'd come! She knew he had Lady Curtis, his god-

mother, staying with him. She understood it was fo
a few days. A lovely woman. Very easy to get alon;
with. But for Casey, there was simply nothing she
could focus on until she saw Troy.

He found her underneath her old ute, her dusty
booted feet sticking out.

"Excuse me," he said. "Would that be Casey
McGuire super-star, under there?"

There was a clatter of tools, a scrape of metal, a
loud curse. "For goodness sake, it's you, Troy!"
She could hardly contain her delight at his arrival.
She was a little mortified, too. Just think how she
looked! In her oldest gear and covered in grease.

She pushed on the trolley sending it scooting out
from under the old ute. "I never expected you."

He studied her, a crooked smile on his face. She
had grease on her nose, her forehead and her
cheeks. Her faded denim shirt had seen much better days. Her jeans had a big hole at one knee. Her
magnificent mane was all but hidden under a scarf
tied pirate fashion around her head. Less said about
her hands the better.

She looked wonderful. "I've just seen Mabs and
Leah off," he said. "They're returning to Sydney. It's
better for Leah. She was very close to Dad. Mabs
will help her through the whole terrible business."

Casey picked up a cloth, wiped her hands. "And

)w are you holding up?" Her eyes narrowed over
im, mesmerised by his male beauty. His face
)oked thinner. Drawn.

"Turns out I feel a whole lot better seeing you. I
)ve the scarf. It's very dashing."

"Beats getting grease in my hair." She whipped the
:carf off, her hair cascading down her back and curl-
ig over her breast. "You came in the helicopter?"

"Yes."

"How did it feel?" she asked with great empathy.

He sighed deeply. "We have to be philosophical
)ut here, Casey. Flying is a way of life. We won't
;et the final report on what happened to Dad and
he Cessna for a while, but at this stage it seems he
night have had a blackout of some sort. A bad turn."

"I thought he was in good health?"

"He never gave any indication otherwise. I sup-
)ose you're in good health until something goes
vrong."

Casey winced involuntarily. "My heart goes out
:o you, Troy. You and Leah. No matter what problems you and your dad had, losing him must be a
great blow."

"It is," Troy said simply. "There I was heading for
a big confrontation about my future and Dad was
leaving this world."

"Don't feel guilty about anything," Casey advised him in a charged voice. "Accept what you

must learn to accept. You loved your dad but yo didn't get on."

"Keep talking," he murmured, blessing the da she had come into his life. "You know I like how yo express yourself. Dad left me Vulcan. Outright."

"Ah, that's good news, Troy," she breathed, fu of relief for him. "I know I didn't make a good im pression on your dad but he looked a man of integ rity. An unhappy man, too. That alone create problems. There didn't seem to be a question abou whether he would do the right thing."

He stared back at her gravely. "I'd like you t come back to Vulcan with me, Casey. Would you I probably won't get the chance to see you again be fore you go back to Sydney. When *are* you going? He struggled not to show the sudden feeling o emptiness.

"I should be there now." She gave a little grimace "Glenn is bursting to move my career along. Tha being said it kinda means I lose my independence. which is something I don't want. Yes, I'll come back with you, Troy. I'll be happy to. You don't look like you've been sleeping much. Maybe you'll fall asleep in my arms."

CHAPTER TEN

WHILE Troy sat and talked to Courtney and Darcy, Casey quickly showered and shampooed her hair, greatly comforted by the realization Troy in his grief wanted to be with her. She dressed in a new blue tank top with an ornamental black zipper down the side. Black sandblast jeans. In the heat her towel-dried hair was a mass of long loose ringlets but she could brush them out. Afterwards she threw a few things into an overnight bag and went downstairs.

"All set?" Darcy looked up with a smile, putting down her cup of coffee.

"Yes." Casey returned the smile, flipping her long hair over her shoulder. "Glenn might ring tonight." She said it apologetically.

"Don't worry. I'll take care of him." Courtney nodded.

"I'll bring Casey back tomorrow, the way I promised." Troy stood to attention. "We should go. I'd like to be back on Vulcan before dusk."

"Take care you two," Darcy said gently, looking from one to the other.

Troy's answering smile was a little bleak.

"I think he's trying to find the strength to give her up," Courtney later confided to her sister.

"If that's what she wants," Darcy answered. "I don't think she does. Troy's a really fine man. I don't think Casey will find many like him. She keeps a lot to herself but it's no secret to *us* anyway she's in love with him."

"I guess it all comes down to whether she wants to focus her entire attention on a career," Courtney said. "It's always like that. Women trying to juggle a career with home and kids. A lot can't manage it. As for me, I was doing okay, but I could never bring myself to give up Adam. Not for anything. I love him."

"Who would doubt it!" Darcy laughed. "Not only that he'll be brought into the family in more ways than one. We need him. Murraree needs him. It couldn't have turned out better. I'm just glad you're allowing me as the eldest to marry first. I don't think we need worry about Casey and Troy," she added calmly. "Both of them are strong people. They'll find a way."

* * *

It was already dark by the time they let themselves in to the homestead, the brilliant violet of dusk vanishing like a puff of smoke.

It was the second time Casey had been inside Vulcan's homestead. The first was after Clifford Connellan's funeral when the house had been jam packed with mourners. Casey hated funerals. They always took her back to the terrible day they had buried her mother. Clifford Connellan's hadn't been so bad. The service wasn't long but it had been uplifting. Everyone who had come from near and far appeared to have had genuine liking and respect for Troy's late father.

Lady Curtis, Troy's godmother, had been a tower of strength. And such a little woman! Casey really appreciated the way Lady Curtis, Troy's "Mabs" had taken the time to catch up with her. Indeed they had had quite a long conversation. It was almost as though Lady Curtis was as protective of her as she obviously was of Troy and Leah. Of course she had been their mother's dearest friend. But that didn't explain why she was so very nice to me, Casey thought. Lady Curtis had as good as ranged herself alongside. Casey had been very grateful.

Once inside, Troy drew her into his arms with a deep sigh. He rested his cheek against hers, then let her go. "There's plenty of food in the house. Let's have a drink first. We can eat later."

"Fine with me." For a big man he was always so tender. "Mind if I wander about?"

He wanted to say my house is your house. All that kept him from saying it was his reluctance to put pressure on her. "Go right ahead," he said. "The house was so crowded the other day. But you'd have seen the general layout. It's not as grand as Murraree now that it's been done up, but I love it. It's *home*. It's where my mother came as a bride."

"You must have photographs of her," Casey said, turning to face him. "I'd love to see them."

Some of the stress on his strongly hewn face drained away. "I'll go and get them. Dad put them away but Leah and I often pull them out."

How awful! Casey thought, shoving precious photographs away in a cabinet. But then it was difficult to judge these things. Bereft people reacted in vastly different ways. Still Elizabeth Connellan's children would have wanted mementos of their mother around. Probably they had photographs of her in their bedrooms. This business of Troy's mother's alleged infidelity had clearly affected him. And yet from what she could make out there was no proof. It could have been a jealous fantasy of his father's. Whatever the answer they'd all suffered. A happy childhood was central to stability in later life. People who'd had that simply didn't know how lucky they were, Casey thought.

My kids are going to have it, she decided, at that point childless.

She wandered into the huge drawing room, looking around her. These cattle barons had made their homes their castles. Vulcan homestead was single storey unlike Murraree but with the same wonderful spacious verandahs. What was *home* to Troy, was very grand to her. Like Murraree the homestead was *huge*. Probably five or six times the size of the average house. And average houses didn't have wonderful paintings on the walls, magnificent chandeliers and splendid furnishings. Not that grand houses made anyone particularly happy. One could be perfectly happy in a cottage. It all came down to where love was.

Troy returned, carrying two leather-bound photo-albums and on top of them a large silver framed studio portrait. He handed it to her.

"My mother." His golden eyes were brilliant. "Elizabeth meet Casey." He made a little ceremony of passing the framed photograph across.

Casey took a deep breath, looking down at the smiling face. "Troy, she's lovely. Absolutely lovely." Sincerity vibrated in her voice. The photograph was black and white but there was no mistaking the luminous eyes, the distinctive arching brows, the thick curling hair, the shapely mouth and that tantalizing smile. "You resemble her greatly," she said softly, rubbing the glass gently with her fingers. "The male version."

"There are a lot more photographs here," Troy said, taking the photo from her and placing it on a marble topped console. "I don't want to bore you stiff. I know it happens. It's happened to me."

"No, I want to see them. I want to know what you were all like."

"All right, you asked for it." He smiled wryly. "Yell out when you've had enough. I think you'll find I was a beautiful child." He managed a mocking grin.

"No happy little shots with you lying naked on your tummy?"

"I hope not. I wouldn't mind seeing one of you, though."

"None of me, Connellan. We didn't own a camera and there were no happy snaps in The Home."

"Why do I always think you capitalize that place?" He led her to a couch and sat down beside her.

"Because I do."

"Why did I bring the bloody place up," Troy chided himself, catching the shadows that chased across her face. "Take a look at this!" He sought to divert her. "It's me on my first pony. I might have been three or four. Are you going to tell me that isn't a beautiful child?"

"I'd like a child like that," Casey said simply.

Heat and adrenaline coursed through his veins. "Then I'm afraid we'd have to get into a steady relationship."

"No affair?" she asked, eyes sparkling, voice bland.

"No way!" He shook his bronze head. "Affairs burn themselves out. I'm talking commitment."

"So am I thank you very much," she said snappily. "You all look so happy." She stared down at the family snap, the fabled Outback floral gardens she had yet to see, as a backdrop. Mother, father, two adorable children. All beaming at the camera. What had ruptured that?

"We were happy. *Then.*" Troy's deep voice was full of regret.

"Your dad could have got it all wrong," she said, turning her head so she could look into his grieving eyes.

His mouth curved down. "Mabs said he did."

"Listen to her if you won't listen to me."

"Who said I don't listen to you?" he retorted. "Hell, McGuire, I live for your every word. Look at this one. Dad and I on a camel. That's me under the too big pith helmet. We've got hundreds of thousands of camels running around the Outback courtesy the Afghans who brought a handful here 150 years ago. Our camels are the healthiest in the world. It's the clean desert environment. They thrive here which isn't real good for our native animals.

They're feral. They compete with our native animal for food and shelter. Plus on heat and it's the male that comes on heat, they can be dangerous critters."

"Can you ride one?" she asked, turning pages slowly.

He made a disgusted sound. "Of course I can. Win races as well. You'll find proof in there." He glanced over her shoulder. "Camels mightn't look it but they're very intelligent animals."

"They make me laugh, that's all. Not that I've actually seen one in the flesh."

"You will," he promised matter-of-factly. "There must be a thousand or more on Vulcan. Feral goats are a problem. They eat almost anything and Outback conditions suit them. Feral cats are worse. They're so destructive. When I'm out on my bore run I couldn't count the number of beautiful birds that have been attacked by feral cats. All they leave is a pile of brilliant feathers. I hate them. All of us on the land do."

"I can understand that. You care about the native animals and the environment. What about the dingoes? I've seen them on Murraree. They breed up in the hills. They're handsome animals."

"They are." He nodded. "Dingo pups are especially beautiful. Bundles of gold. As long as their numbers are controlled we don't have a problem with our native dog. They can't bark, you know. They howl."

She gave a little shiver. "I know. I've heard them. It's so mournful."

"They're only locating their mates or their pups." He pointed to a magnificent shot of two horsemen chasing brumbies. "I'm the first rider. The other one was our foreman. A great bloke. He was killed by a feral pig. If you ever see one get right out of the way. They're one of the dangerous critters.

"Had enough?" he asked, watching her. The temptation to pull her into his arms was almost overwhelming. But he'd decided he was going to do nothing to hurry her in any way.

"No." She started on the second album. All these family photographs brought him closer to her. In the second album there were fewer photos of Leah as she no doubt moved away to city life. His mother no longer featured, either. There were photographs of polo meets. In several Troy, Curt Berenger and another handsome guy she didn't know had their arms thrown around one another's necks, grinning widely. She saw his eyes close in pain at the shots of the family Cessna with he and his father and sometimes Leah standing alongside.

"You know Dad had been flying well over thirty years without incident," he confided in a hollow voice. "I keep dwelling on what his last moments must have been like."

She reached out, curled her fingers around his.

"Maybe it was as they say. Your whole life runs on fast forward before your eyes. He would have been thinking of you and Leah. He would have been thinking of his wife."

"I don't think he ever stopped loving her." Strong emotion was hidden under harshness. "Though he often used to say loving weakens a man."

"That's because he couldn't bear his loss. I don't know if you believe in an afterlife, but I do. It's the only way I could accept the brutal loss of my mother. I would see her again. If you try a little, Troy, I think you'll be able to picture your mother and father together. If there's a Heaven that's where love pours down like sunshine."

"That's beautiful, McGuire," he said, picking up her hand and kissing it.

They ate in the cool of the rear terrace with the stars blossoming huge as diamond daisies in a dark purple sky.

Casey decided his face looked a little more relaxed now. Obviously he'd been giving himself hell. She guessed he had been struggling under a tremendous weight of guilt as well as grief since he had intended having a showdown with his father when he returned. Except it didn't turn out that way. Clifford Connellan had not survived the flight.

She'd made the simple meal and served it. Peppered steaks and a green salad. From the way he bent his head to it Casey decided either it looked very good or he hadn't had the stomach to eat up to date. At any rate, he polished it off so she served another course of tinned peaches and vanilla ice cream. She was no Courtney in the kitchen but neither of them had any trouble disposing of the meal.

Troy made the coffee. Good coffee. They took it back outdoors. A cooling breeze was blowing in from the desert, ruffling her hair. She loved the sweet and the spicy aromatic scents that gusted towards them, released by the night air.

"That was good. I enjoyed it," Troy complimented her, allowing his eyes to drink her in. The soft exterior lights bathed her, turning her hair into a glory. There was every hue of rich gold, red-gold and copper. Her eyes were like jewels. Her full lips under the small straight nose were curved in a teasing smile.

"That's because you're hungry. I'm a lousy cook."

He shook his head. "I can't accept that, McGuire. The steak was cooked to perfection and the salad had a bite."

"Thai dressing," she said.

"When we clear up here, there's another thing you have to do for me." A corner of his mouth turned up at the change in her expression. "I haven't finished yet."

"I assure you sex wasn't on my mind," she said and coloured.

"For as long as I've known you it's never been off mine. But that wasn't what I was going to say. I want you to sing for me. Would you? Please."

Casey caught the ripple of emotion in his luminous eyes. "You really want me to?"

The need for comfort only she could bring was a driving force. "Why should that surprise you? I love your voice. Your speaking voice and the way you sing. It reaches me. Right in here." He struck a spot on his broad chest.

"You need *soothing*," she said.

My God, didn't he! The last few days had been terrible. Now it seemed like a miracle they were alone together.

They had cleared the table, done the dishes, Troy had fetched Leah's abandoned guitar, now they were back in the drawing room. Troy was lounging on a sofa, his long legs stretched out in front of him. Casey was seated on a brocade covered bench tuning the guitar. A very good one, though as it turned out Leah had lacked the talent or the commitment or both to give it much use.

"Ready yourself for a new song," she said softly, her sapphire gaze full of pure emotion. It lingered on his marvellous face, lost itself in his golden eyes.

Her gaze still on him she plucked out the introduction—then began to croon, using a free rhythm.

"It's a little hard gettin' used to this idea of loving,
I mean I found precious little lovin' in my life
It's a little hard getting used to tenderness and attention,
tenderness and attention are things I've never had
Then along came you
Not part of my world
Yet you found that still quiet place inside me not touched since long ago
You made me love you
You know you did
You understood all about me
I'm not alone now in my own skin
You made me love you
You're part of all that I am
You made me love you
You know you did
I carry you around every single minute of ever single hour of every
single day
You're part of me, part of the woman I've become
Love can make or break us
But life has changed direction
Just when I thought my ties to happiness were all but cut away.

The circle of your arms around me is just like
coming home.
For you are what I long for
What I long have sought
For you, for you, are the meaning to my life.

She half spoke the last few words, then gently set
down the guitar. "What do you think? I can polish it.
It was more or less ad lib." Her eyes scanned his face.

He was so unbearably moved he had to take a
moment to answer. Who the hell had laid down in
stone a strong man shouldn't cry? "What do I
think?" Starkly he realised the extent of her talent.
"Casey, come here to me." He spread his large
hands, gathered her into him, while she settled her
head on his shoulder. "I love it. The lyrics and the
haunting melody. It was beautiful. I can't think it
needs polishing at all." He kissed her warm silky
head beneath his chin. "I had the feeling it was
about me. About us. Is that right?" His tone of voice
begged for it to be true.

"Would it trouble you if I loved you?" She sat perfectly still.

"Trouble me!" His voice was rough with invad-
ing emotions. "I'm so shook up I can't adequately
express my emotions. They're like an avalanche."

"Yet you're troubled it mightn't work? You and
me?" She tipped her head to stare into his face, lov-

ing the fact it was so close she could see the fine grain of his skin.

"You could leave me when you've had enough." His heart dropped like a stone. "God knows I can't cage you, or your talent. That would be wrong. Gifts like yours are meant to be used."

He waited for her to answer. She said nothing

"Whatever happens, Casey, it's been worth *everything!*"

It was an admission that came from the heart. Yet something flashed across her face. A hint of rebellion. "You could *have* me yet you seem to be offering me a way out?" she challenged, feeling like a door was opening only to be shut in her face.

His laugh was abrupt. "For God's sake, that's the *last* thing I want. How can you doubt it? I want to keep you close to me always. I have dreams, too, Casey."

"But you question my ability to be part of them?" She let her flash of anger show. She who had suffered so much rejection.

"Hey, settle down." His arm travelled back and forth across her back, gentling her like she was a temperamental filly. "I'll never be able to forget you're a redhead, will I? What I'm saying is, I'm scared as all hell what I can offer you mightn't be enough. I couldn't bear it if we married and you left me some time in the future. Divorced me. It happens."

"You're afraid of hurt?"

"Not hurt. Desolation," he said quietly. "Aren't you?"

Her expression changed as her spirit opened wider. She let out a sigh. "I'm sorry, Troy. I know we have to talk this out, but I'm getting ruled by my emotions. You've touched me like nobody else can. You're worried my career will become more important to me as time goes by?"

"It scares me," he said succinctly. "Your music is so much a part of you."

"It is. But what you seem to be talking about is performances. Going away on tour?"

"Heck yes!" He nodded his head sharply. "I'm absolutely certain that's what Gardiner has in mind. I hear on all sides you've got a big future. I firmly believe it. What hope would I have, Casey, girl, keeping you down on the farm?"

"You could keep me pregnant," she suggested, not bothering to rein in her emotion. "I'd like four kids."

"Casey, honey, be serious," he begged, grasping a thick knot of her hair and holding her beautiful face up to him.

"You don't want kids?" She pressed her lips together.

He gave in to his helpless desire to kiss her, taking his time about it. "We could start tonight seeing you're in such a hurry," he muttered, desperate to leave his imprint on her. "I want kids nearly as much as I want *you!*"

"Well I want kids so much it *hurts,*" she moaned. "I've already planned on your being the father. Of course if you reckon a strong woman is too much to handle—"

He gave a harsh guffaw. "I'd be happy to tame you, McGuire."

"That's good!" she sighed voluptuously, her breasts swelling, "because I'm desperate to be made love to."

Sensual heat was in his hands. "I can help you with that, too." Isn't that what love was? he thought. Laying himself open to everything, including pain?

She brushed a tear from her lashes. "Your father's dead, yet we go on with life."

"We *have* to," he said, his heart jolted with fresh pain.

"Your dad didn't like me much," she said in a melancholy voice.

"So how come he described you as a glorious creature?"

She stared up at him, her eyebrows rising in disbelief. "I'm amazed to hear that." Clifford Connellan *could not* have said it the way he'd looked at her.

"It's true all the same." Troy laughed strangely. "That was Dad. He couldn't seem to say anything good to your face." He stood, bringing her with him. "I've waited for you *forever!* You're like the light at the end of a long dark tunnel."

"I like that!" she sighed. "It's true for me, too. I'm here now, Troy," she soothed him, revelling in the love he communicated just holding her in his arms. "And I won't be gone in the morning, either. We're going to wake up together. It'll be wonderful! You said you loved my song. *Think* what I was saying. It was about *us.* Not just another song for an album. I love you, Troy. I want to share my life with you. *That's* my ambition."

Elation fell on him like gold dust. He drew back a moment to rest his hands on her shoulders. "The world lost for love, Casey?" His eyes touched her lovely mouth. "As long as you're very, very *sure?*"

"*You* are my fulfilment, Connellan," she said huskily. "None of it matters but you."

His body, which had been knotted with tension, relaxed. "Truly?"

"You bet!" She shaped the words fiercely lest he doubt her. "Though I'm disappointed you couldn't trust me a little. As for my career! I don't long for success in that way. Besides." She shrugged. "There's nothing stopping me from continuing to write songs."

He smiled crookedly. "I'd thought that myself." How many times had he thought it? He'd even tried to steer her towards it. But would it be enough?

Her heart melted at the hope in his eyes. "Have you forgotten I'll have other things occupying my time? I've thought about this, Troy, just the way you have. No matter what Glenn has in mind I never intended to jump on the merry-go-round. I've made a lot of useful contacts. I know people in the business. There's no reason why I can't get my songs out there without making a career the entire focus of my life. It's not a big deal cutting albums, either. Maybe a personal appearance now and again. I'm sure it could be worked out and if it can't? I'll still be okay. I'll have *you!*"

"You sure will." His arms closed around her. "I'm your man. But you can't just drop everything, can you?" Troy was desperate to make this work. "You signed a contract."

"Yes and Adam vetted it. He made sure he looked after my interests. I haven't signed my life away. Be sure of that."

Troy clung to that. He had been offered this one chance at heaven. He wasn't about to let it slip out of reach. "Then the sooner I get a ring on your finger the better," he said.

If it pleased her he would love her to wear his mother's ring. Sapphire for the colour of her eyes. Diamonds for the sparkle. The earrings. The necklace. Surely his father must have known?

Ring! For some incredibly strange reason Casey

hadn't reckoned on rings. Her mother didn't have
any engagement ring. Wedding ring, either. Destiny
had robbed her of that.

Almost in a trance Casey allowed him to lead her
into his bedroom where he suddenly swooped her
up into his arms like a doll and laid her on the bed.
The look on his face, the passion and the vibrancy
almost knocked her out.

Never had she been more aware of herself as a
woman. A woman *loved.* Every nerve in her body
had electricity running through it. Tears pricked in
her eyes, gathered. Transforming tears that came
from the deepest depths of her being. No wonder
he was filled with fear she might leave him. Her
only wish now was never to leave his side. She
was quite clear in her mind what her goal was. He
was bigger, better, more generous, more compassionate than any man she had ever known. And he
was *hers!* This wasn't some impossible dream. It
was a living experience and it was happening now.

Troy! A lion among men with his unblinking
golden gaze.

It was trained on her, so desirous, so tender, *de-
vout!* How beautiful, how humbling. In utter silence he undressed her, unravelling and peeling her
like a peach, running his hands lingeringly up and
down the trembling length of her body, hands vi-
brating over her breasts, her stomach, her mound,

his callused fingertips so erotic. Pleasure and excitement rippled across her face. Her eyelids were fluttering. She strained upward towards him and he swooped, kissing her.

Then swiftly he turned away shucking his clothes to reveal his own superb body, his skin many many shades deeper than hers. Bronze velvet, white satin.

She called to him in an excited whisper and he went to her, all his senses ablaze, his throat crowded with words of love but too dry to say them. The two of them melted into each other like wax melts in flames. It was a meeting not just of the physical, but the emotional and the spiritual. It was a declaration of love that was to prove as constant as a rock.

They were alone. Perfectly alone, each striving to hold on to the solemnity of this night. Something that could be forever recalled. Casey had no other name for her rapture than perfection.

How to hold on to it?

She knew how.

Grasp it with both hands.

EPILOGUE

Murraree Station
The Once in a Lifetime Wedding
Of Darcy McIvor & Curt Berenger

ON THIS day of all days the bride looked exquisite, lit from within. The love she felt for her husband shimmered in her remarkable aquamarine eyes. Joy radiated from her to him, spilling over onto their families and their many happy guests. The elegant simplicity of her bridal gown, a rich duchesse satin, set off Darcy's own natural beauty and her regal air.

She was attended by four bridesmaids, her sisters, Courtney and Casey and her friends from childhood Fiona Kinsella and Lisa Sanders. The bridesmaids, too, wore duchesse satin. But whereas the bride favoured a high neck and fitted sleeves, the bridesmaids' gowns were strapless, form fitting with a removable train. The colours were lovely; harmonising shades of violet, jacaranda, cerise and

ose-pink. Each colour suited the wearer perfectly.
Around their young throats they wore a lustrous
necklet of Broome pearls, the finest in the world,
each pearl perfectly matched to its neighbour. Gifts
from the bridegroom to be treasured forever.

The searing heat of the Dry was over. The tropical North had received weeks of torrential rain,
causing the flood waters to rush down every
drought ravaged river and stream. A thousand miles
away the vast flat bed of interlocking waterways
that was the Channel Country became the catch-
ment area for the life giving rains.

After the water abated there was rich fattening
pasture for the cattle, the Outback animals and the
great legions of birds, particularly the nomadic water
birds that flocked in to the brimming swamps and
billabongs to breed. The paper-dry red earth seemingly overnight became a monumental carpet of ev-
erlastings, white, gold, pink and purple. The scarlet
Sturt Desert Pea spread for miles like a luxuriant
rampant vine. Native orchids made their brief, rav-
ishing appearance, the sun orchids, the slipper orchids and the enamel orchids with their glossy petals.

Prostrate desert plants flowered in vast patches,
the Carpet of Snow, the Firebush, the Saltbush and
the yellow poppies while on the hill country bank
after bank of green pussytails and lilac. Lambs'
tails smothered the ancient rubble and waved in the

breeze. A breeze that was scented with a billio
wildflowers, with the lovely top note, the sweetl
fragrant native boronia.

Everyone celebrating on Murraree that day had
prayed for rain. No one more so than the bride. Darcy
wanted the miracle of the wildflowers for her wed
ding day. It was the most fortuitous omen. She
wanted her sisters, Courtney and Casey to experience
the short lived, but unforgettable glory. She wanted
the wedding party to have their photos taken amid
the desert splendour. It seemed like a fairy tale to
Darcy her sisters were well on their way to experiencing the swelling joy, the utter bliss that came with
marriage to the man one loved with all one's heart.

Courtney wore Adam's ring with pride. Casey
more happy than she ever dreamed, wore Troy's.
Both were already planning their weddings. Courtney first. Casey next.

But first they have to recover from mine! cried
Darcy's inner voice in an explosion of joy.

The reception was held in great marquees in the
grounds. A veritable feast! It was all just so perfect
no one wanted it to end. But of course it had to end.
There was always tomorrow. Darcy McIvor-Beren-
ger was embarking on a new life. There were
speeches, lots of speeches, some that brought laughter, some that brought a tear. More luminous tears
when the time came for bride and groom to make

their departure. Six weeks had been set aside for the honeymoon. Two on a very beautiful Great Barrier Reef island, a secluded paradise, that attracted people who sought privacy. The month after they were to fly to Paris, the most romantic city in the world. The city for lovers.

It was Casey, gloriously statuesque in violet who caught the bridal bouquet simply by raising her arm. She couldn't see for a moment how gorgeous it was because her sapphire eyes were blurred with tears.

"You know what that means, don't you?" Troy murmured in her ear, secretly thrilled they could be next.

"Yes!" She gulped for air. "I'm the tallest bridesmaid."

And the most beautiful Troy thought, encircling her narrow waist and drawing her back into his warm embrace. His eyes locked momentarily with Adam's. Adam was a nice guy. They got on well. Both young men exchanged happy smiles.

Courtney, like a porcelain figurine in her rose-pink satin dress stood just in front of Adam, as high as his heart. Her tears were melting into laughter at something he had said. The other bridesmaids in high spirits were laughing with guests, their slender arms aloft. One after the other the bridesmaids had all embraced Darcy. Now everyone was waving at the station vehicle that was taking bride and groom to the airstrip where Curt's Beech Baron was waiting to fly them to Brisbane, the State capital, the first leg of their trip. Curt's best man was running beside the vehicle but gradually he had to fall back, still waving.

Marian in yellow silk and an amazingly pretty hat looked every inch the proud mother of the bride. She stood a little distance away with her second husband, Peter, who had brought her into a calm harbour with a tranquillity she had never had.

There you are, Jock. See what you missed. Three beautiful daughters.

Darcy, Courtney, Casey. Father to each. Darcy who you caused to remain at your side in isolation. Courtney who you allowed to go with me, the wife you betrayed. Casey, child of a forbidden love, who lost her own tragic mother and was imprisoned in an orphanage.

Well Jock, they've all triumphed. Their lives have come together.

Marian had the unshakable certainty the bond was unbreakable.

They were all in their way, McIvor Women.

HARLEQUIN®
Presents

The world's bestselling romance series...
The series that brings you your favorite authors,
month after month:

Helen Bianchin...Emma Darcy
Lynne Graham...Penny Jordan
Miranda Lee...Sandra Marton
Anne Mather...Carole Mortimer
Susan Napier...Michelle Reid

and many more uniquely talented authors!

Wealthy, powerful, gorgeous men...
Women who have feelings just like your own...
The stories you love, set in exotic, glamorous locations...

HARLEQUIN®
Presents

Seduction and Passion Guaranteed!

HPDIR104

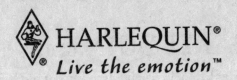
HARLEQUIN®
Live the emotion™

Upbeat,
All-American Romances

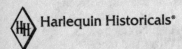
Romantic Comedy

Historical,
Romantic Adventure

Romantic Suspense

The essence of
modern romance

Seduction and passion
guaranteed

Emotional,
Exciting, Unexpected

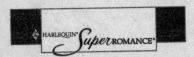

Sassy, Sexy, Seductive!